LEGEND
OF
SERPENTINE

THE LOST KINGDOM

MARC-ANTHONY COOK

ATLAS ELITE
PUBLISHING
PARTNERS

Cover Design by: Michael Beas

Printed in the United States of America

First Edition: November 2024

Dedication

To my dad,

Looking back over the past two years of writing this novel, I see you in every step of my process. Your unwavering support, boundless patience, and endless encouragement have guided me through the highs and lows of making my idea a reality. This book is a testament to the values you have instilled in me to never give up on my dreams and the love you've always shown. Thank you for believing in me every step of the way.

With all my love,
Marc-Anthony

Thunderfang

This species is one of the strongest species that live on this island.

They have the power to control the element of energy, the most common form being lightning.

They can be a wide variety of colors, though each color is believed to resemble how they act.

While most have a regular snakelike tail, those considered "royalty" are born with a razor sharp spike at the end of their tails.

They can normally only control lightning, though there is thought to be a birth defect that gives the dragonet an extra talent.

Their current whereabouts are unknown

Dune Scorpion

These ferocious arachnids live in the dry desert areas of the island, and seem to control the element of sand and stone.

They seem to have a strange militaristic behavior when it comes to territory.

These beasts can grow to be around the size of a large elephant, and have two tails, each with a highly venomous barb that has the ability to turn their prey into stone.

They seem to follow a king of sorts, which is whomever is the largest of the bunch.

They have the ability to harden their claws on command to the point where they are practically indestructible.

Fire Nymph

These are highly unpredictable creatures that seem to have control over fire.

They can be found living in groups around an active volcano on the far east of the island.

These creatures resemble humans but with large wispy trails of smoke instead of legs and fiery hot wings.

They are a mostly peaceful species, but when threatened, they will gather together and unleash wave after wave of blistering hot air and fire at their attacker.

This is the only species that humans have made successful contact and friendship with, and they have become great allies.

Ice Giants

These creatures can be found in the frozen tundra on the west side of the island.

As the name suggests, these beings are able to control the element of ice.

These beasts are incredibly powerful, but are also dimwitted, so they are not a threat on their own.

Ice Giants can communicate using sign language, like apes, and are willing to follow whatever they see as the strongest thing in the area.

They are rather shy creatures and have not tried to move beyond the icy glaciers they call home.

Leviathan

These massive eel-like creatures dwell in the vast oceans that surround the island.

They are extremely territorial, preferring a more solo lifestyle.

They have control over the element of water and use this to slice through the water at tremendous speeds.

Their massive tails can current strong currents and massive waves that revenge the seas and shores.

There has only been one documented case where a leviathan has tried to get onto land.

Heavenly Wisp

Very little is known about these majestic birds, as they spend most of their lives high in the clouds.

They are believed to have control of the element of air and wind, creating the clouds that float above our island.

These birds seem to have wings made purely of the clouds that surround them.

Serpentine Isle

CONTENTS

Prologue 1

Chapter 1 5

Chapter 2 17

Chapter 3 28

Chapter 4 37

Chapter 5 48

Chapter 6 58

Chapter 7 70

Chapter 8 78

Chapter 9 90

Chapter 10... 102

Chapter 11... 115

Chapter 12... 121

Chapter 13... 126

Chapter 14... 136

Chapter 15... 144

Chapter 16... 155

Chapter 17... 164

Epilogue 172

PROLOGUE

Four people sat around at a campfire, eating smores, singing songs, and having fun under a beautiful sunset. It was a mother and father, and their two kids, who had decided to go camping for the week.

"Dad, can you tell us a story?" asked one of the kids, looking up expectantly at the father.

"Hmm, I don't know, it's getting kind of late." the father said, starting to get up.

"Pleease, we promise we'll be good." the other kid begged, looking at the father.

"Oh alright, I guess I can tell you one story." the father said, sitting back down and looking at the two kids. "Hmm, let's see here... oh! I know." the father said, thinking out loud.

Our story begins long, long ago, on this very island, which remains hidden from the rest of the world. An island full of mystical and magical creatures that have the ability to harness the elements of the world. Wind... ice... water... fire... earth, and the one that rose above all others... lightning.

These elements and the creatures that used them lived at peace with each other, until a great war swept across the island . All of a sudden, the tribes started wanting more and more. They started killing others to try to steal their powers. These tribes broke apart into six different regions of the island. The fire nymphs took over the volcanic hills, the heavenly wisps took to the skies, the ice giants fled to the frozen tundra, the leviathans disappeared deep under the waves, and the dune scorpions fled to the desert.

The only creatures that did not flee were the thunderfangs, the masters of lightning. They held their ground and tried to stop the senseless slaughter. Eventually, they succeeded at bringing the tribes back together and they were beginning to bring peace once more to their island. But, after a few years, the thunderfangs got a new queen, SnowStorm. She was a good queen for a while and had three eggs.

But over time she became as wicked as a creature could get and only wanted power. Her husband, King WhirlWind, tried to convince her to stop her evil and wicked ways. In an outrage she attacked him and brought him to the brink of death. WhirlWind had to use an ancient artifact, an amulet of sorts, to defeat her. One that could harness the powers of the other elements.

He was able to use this artifact to defeat SnowStorm and seal her in a block of ice, hoping she would never break free. Sadly WhirlWind died soon after because the amulet had drained him of the last bit of energy he had left. When the palace guards found them they were ordered to hide the three eggs far far away, in case anyone tried to destroy them and erase the royal bloodline.

These eggs were left untouched and hidden for hundreds of years as the war started to pick back up and continue to rage on. Then in a time we call, the era of the redeemed, those eggs hatched. From those eggs came three dragonets, the hero of our story, Bolt, dark with underscales that glowed the color of lightning, The second dragonet, Rose, hatched two years later dark pink with underscales that glowed a bright vibrant pink and a joyful aura. But as we all know nothing comes out perfect, the third egg hatched a year before Rose. The egg had a darkened shell and radiated a dark energy.

This egg hatched and a midnight black dragonet came out with blood red eyes and underscales, Fury. Years went by and Bolt grew up to be a brave warrior, loyal, steadfast, and kind, Rose grew up to be the meaning of peace, pure of heart and always happy, and Fury grew up twisted and dark like his mother, an outcast and a villain. These three dragonets would be the very future of our island, and if all went well they would bring our little island out of hiding, into the world for others to see, without fear of being cast out, feared, and hated.

But, if things were to go wrong and something happened to these dragonets, it would spell disaster for not only our island but the rest of the world as we know it, for evil would finally overcome good and the world would plunge into darkness, annihilating everything in its path.

CHAPTER

I

"Just a little bit closer..."Bolt said quietly, as he and his sister snuck up behind a large goat. Bolt preferred to hunt alone, he found it much easier to sneak up on prey when you only had to worry about keeping yourself quiet. But Bolt had decided to bring his sister, Rose, because he thought that she would like to spend some time outside of their cave. Bolt came to a stop when he heard his sister begin to speak. They were so close, and Bolt began to worry that Rose might scare off the goat, making things a lot harder for the two of them if they had to track it down again.

"Are you sure we have to kill it?"Rose whispered, frowning at Bolt. Bolt slowly turned to face his sister, trying to make as little noise as he could before responding.

"You do want dinner today, right?" Bolt replied to his little sister with a smirk. "We won't be having anything for dinner if you scare away that goat." Rose let out a little sigh and nodded her head. "That's what I thought." Bolt said, as he went back to slowly creeping up behind the goat. While they had been talking, the goat had moved further away from them. Bolt pressed his entire body as flat as he could on the ground and snuck closer to the goat to where it would be in striking distance. Bolt lunged forward towards the goat, wrapping his powerful body around the unsuspecting animal, coil after coil.

The goat made a loud bleat of panic as Bolt began to squeeze the air out of its lungs.

Rose let out a little whimper and quickly looked away from the gruesome scene. She didn't want to watch as Bolt continued to squeeze the life out of the unfortunate creature. She didn't dare look back as she heard the recognizable loud cracking as the goats bones began to break. Rose only looked back when everything went quiet, seeing the limp body of the goat. Bolt slowly began to unwind from the goat and gave her a satisfied smile.

"That had to have been the largest goat I've seen around here in quite some time. It really was a great catch wasn't it?" Bolt said with a smile. He waited for some sort of response, but his sister said nothing. Bolt looked at Rose, and sighed, seeing her uneasy expression.

"Look, I know killing other creatures isn't something you enjoy doing, but we've got to eat, you do understand that, right?" he said with a little smile, trying to do whatever he could to make her feel even the slightest bit better.

"Why can't we just have fruit like we did yesterday?" Rose sighed and looked up at her brother with a hopeful expression. Bolt couldn't keep his smile from getting bigger as he saw his little sister's pleading expression.

"I'm bored of fruit, we've had nothing but fruit for the past three days because of you!" Bolt replied with an exasperated sigh. "But, if that's what you want to have instead, I guess I can find something for you to eat." He sighed, shaking his head in frustration.

"Thank you! Thank you! Thank you!" Rose said excitedly with a big grin on her face, her tail wagging around excitedly.

Bolt wrapped his tail around the dead goat and dragged it with him to go and find his sister something to eat.

"Fury wouldn't have asked for fruit. Who am I kidding, he wouldn't have asked for anything, he would have just taken whatever he wanted." Bolt grumbled under his breath. Bolt immediately winced at the thought of his little brother, quiet and angry, always staying in the deep recesses in their cave.

He used to be so normal, but over these past few years it's like he's growing away from us. Now he just tries to stay as far away from us as he can. He thought to himself. Bolt shook his head to try and keep the wave of memories from washing over him. *What was I doing again? Right, I was going to go and find something for Rose to eat.* He thought, pushing down all of his sappy feelings.

I think I saw some mango trees not too far from here last time I patrolled around this area. I'll get Rose some of those. Bolt went off deeper into the jungle, in the direction of the mango trees, muttering to himself along the way. When he had finally gotten to the trees, something immediately felt off, different somehow.

He stopped and began to look around, slowly getting more and more confused by what he saw. It looked like the plants around the area had been trampled down by something.

That's strange? He thought, getting a closer look at the plants. *I don't remember there being any animals that lived in this spot. The only thing near here is a small group of strange little critters, but even then I hardly think those small creatures would risk wandering in the jungle, when about everything could kill a creature their size.* Bolt always memorized the area around him, capturing every little detail in his mind, so it was unusual for him to miss something as obvious as this. While Bolt was thinking, he heard a twig snap in the distance. Bolt tilted his head, picking up on a little scuttle he heard in the bushes a couple yards away. He looked up, startled, and immediately became alert, as he continued looking in the direction of which the noise had come from.

"Who's there!?" he hissed, flicking his forked tongue out, trying to detect what had made the noise. Bolt reared back to make himself look bigger to try and scare off whatever was making the noise. There was no response, just the sound of the leaves rustling in the wind.

Must have just been a rabbit or something. He thought to himself with a sigh, trying to calm his nerves before looking around again just to be safe. No matter how hard he tried to relax he just couldn't shake the feeling that he was being watched. He decided to try a little trick he discovered a few weeks ago when he had to scare off a group of unusually large bears that were getting too close to their cave.

Bolt coiled his tail up into a small tight spiral, then he quickly flicked out his tail like a whip. There was a loud crack like thunder as the spike on his tail let out a flurry of sparks from the motion.

That should have scared off whatever might have been watching me, if anything was really watching me. Bolt thought, his mind beginning to ease. After a while his stomach began to growl loudly, as if it was trying to remind him of why he was here in the first place.

I should head back now. I guess I can also try to find something for Fury on my way back, even though I think he should have come out hunting with me so he could find something for himself.

Bolt grabbed a few of the mangoes from the trees, looking around the trees one final time and cautiously began to head back the way he came from, looking behind him every now and then to see if he was being followed. *Something was watching me, I just don't know what. Just in case, I will warn Rose to stay away from this area for a while. She's not going to like that though.* He thought, letting out an exasperated sigh.

When Bolt finally returned to where he had left Rose, he had a few mangoes tucked under his wings and a second goat he had managed to catch for Fury held in his jaws.

"Well, what did you get me?" Rose asked excitedly with a curious expression, looking around and trying to figure out what her brother had gotten for her. Bolt dropped the goat and looked back up at Rose with a smile.

"I thought I would get you some mangoes from the trees farther back in the jungle, since I know you like them." Bolt grinned, lifting one of his wings and showing her the mangoes.

"And I'm sure getting those was such a hassle for you." Rose giggled, teasing her brother. Bolt let out a small laugh, smiling at his sister.

"This might come as a surprise to you, but it was actually quite easy." Bolt replied in a silly manner. Then a serious expression slowly began to fall upon his face.

"Although, something did feel very wrong though, so I don't want you to go back there until I can make sure everything is fine."

"Ugh, but that could take days!" Rose whined, looking down and pouting. "That's one of my favorite spots. It's one of the only places I have left that's truly quiet and peaceful."

"It's for your own safety. I want you to promise to me that you won't go back there until I say it's alright." Bolt said scornfully.

"But!" Rose insisted, beginning to protest.

"Promise." Bolt repeated, looking straight into her eyes with a serious expression.

"Fine, I promise." Rose mumbled sourly with a frown.

"Good. Now, I think we should head back home before our brother gets too cranky." Bolt said, picking up the goat and mangoes and taking off into the sky. Rose followed, close behind him, her bad attitude quickly disappearing as she started doing little tricks in the air.

The two of them flew back in the direction of their cave. Their cave wasn't much, but it was large enough to keep them well hidden and more importantly, safe. It had a beautiful view of the large, mountainous landscape, a beautiful jungle that surrounded them. Their cave also had a little stream that flowed throughout their cave that they used to play in when they were younger. As Bolt was flying, he began to look at the area around them, taking it all in with a satisfied sigh.

I have always wondered what it would be like out there, in a big open area, instead of in a creepy cave, away from everyone else. Bolt thought, as they got to the entrance of the cave. No sooner had they entered the cave, did they hear the snarling voice of their brother.

"What took you so long?" Fury hissed, slowly approaching the two of them, the spike on his tail glowing and twitching dangerously.

"Oh calm down!" Bolt snapped with a slight hiss in his voice. "We would have been home faster if you had actually come with us instead of sulking around all day and getting angry at anything that moved!" Bolt moved up in front of his brother. "I could have gotten you nothing you know." He hissed. "But I did anyway." Bolt glared at his brother, holding the two goats.

Fury scoffed and snatched the largest goat from his brother, devouring it instantly. Bolt let out another hiss and dropped the mangoes. He brought the other goat he had caught and moved away from his brother.

"Can't even manage a thank you." He hissed, glaring at Fury. Seeing the tension between the two, Rose grabbed one of the mangoes and moved up in between her two brothers to try and ease the tension between the two.

"You know, you two really shouldn't be arguing with each other. We're a family, which means we have to stick together no matter what." She said with a big smile as Bolt started eating. She took a bite of her mango and looked back up at the two of them, wiping the juice off of her snout.

"Some family y'all are." Fury snarled. "I would have been better off alone." He hissed, wincing as Rose quickly pricked him with the spike on her tail.

"Well then maybe you should leave! Go on, go be alone, I won't try to stop you!" Bolt roared at his brother. Rose jabbed at him with her tail and glared at him.

"Fine, I guess I agree with her." Bolt said sourly, looking at his sister and then back at his brother, before taking another bite of his goat.

"And what about you?" Rose asked, looking at Fury with a smug grin. Fury let out a low growl and rolled his eyes. "I'll take that as a yes." She said with a smirk, before taking another bite of her mango. After they had finished eating, Fury went back into the shadows and curled up, drifting off into a dreamless sleep.

Letting out a sigh, Bolt went to his favorite spot in their cave. A little ledge on the wall, with a small hole above it which had weathered away over time.

During the day the sun would shine through the hole, illuminating the cave, filling it with a warm light. During the night, the moonlight would shine through the hole while he was sleeping, making his scales shimmer and glow.

Bolt laid down on the ledge, curling up with his head resting on his tail. The day's events flowed through his mind as he slowly started drifting into a deep sleep as well. No sooner had he fallen asleep, he felt something poking at his side. Slowly opening his eyes, he saw his sister in front of him, her tail shaking with excitement.

"Do you think we could go look at the jungle lights tonight?" she asked, the energy inside of her rising as her tail started shaking faster.

Bolt let out a yawn and looked at Rose with tired eyes. "No. For two reasons, the first one being it's not even midnight, so the jungle wouldn't be glowing and full of life yet.

"Two, it's dangerous out there. There could be others who would want to take over that part of the island and I don't think we're ready to defend ourselves if we are attacked."

"Ugh, fine, you're no fun." Rose pouted and curled up beside him. Bolt smiled at his sister as she slowly began to fall asleep again with a yawn.

"Goodnight sis." He whispered with a smile as he looked down at her. His head rose, spotting his brother, who was twitching in his sleep. "Goodnight Fury." He sighed as he laid his head back down and fell into a deep sleep.

"Bolt...Bolt..." Bolt slowly opened his eyes and saw nothing but darkness all around him. "Bolt!" an unfamiliar voice shouted, seeming to come from the shadows.

"Who's there!?" Bolt hissed, quickly getting up, his spiked tail crackling with electricity, his throat glowing as he prepared to let out a burst of lightning. Whoever this was, Bolt was ready to give them the shock of a lifetime.

The voice let out a calm chuckle. "I see you have no hesitation in getting ready for a fight. You must have gotten that from me."

"Who are you?" Bolt hissed, but let his guard down a bit, surprised by how calm the speaker sounded.

"Oh, you don't know who I am? I guess that's reasonable, since the last time I saw you, you were still an egg."

Bolt tilted his head a bit confused and repeated the question. "Who are you? Where have you taken me?" he asked, a little bit more nervous.

"Calm down, you are still in your cave, with the little one fast asleep beside you." The voice replied in a calming tone.

Now Bolt was really confused. "Do you mean Rose? Have you been spying on us!?" He hissed, his eyes straining as he tried to spot whomever was talking to him.

"You need to calm down, you're asleep, and if you get too worked up you'll wake up before we can finish our conversation." The voice said in a calm tone.

"Wait, are you telling me this is all a dream? I've never had a dream like this before." Bolt asked, completely lost about what was going on.

"There is something I must show you." The voice said in a serious tone. Suddenly the darkness began to break away and Bolt found himself in front of a large palace, which was burning to the ground. Bolt gasped and moved back as he looked at the carnage in horror.

"Where am I now? What happened here?" he asked, the fear showing in his voice.

"Do not worry, it's not real," The voice said calmly. "It's your old home, the palace, where you should have grown up, and this is only a glimpse of what will happen if you don't hurry." Now Bolt's entire body was shaking from fear.

"Hurry? Hurry for what!?" Bolt asked in a panicked voice.

"You can't spend the rest of your life in this cave. It's time for you to go out into the world and face the challenges that come your way. You must save our home and the few of us who still live there." The voice insisted with urgency, ignoring Bolt's question.

Suddenly everything disappeared as Bolt was jostled awake by his sister. Rose had a worried look on her face as she looked down at Bolt, with Fury beside her, looking at him with an annoyed expression.

"Finally you're awake." His brother huffed scowling at him, before slowly backing away.

"We were so worried about you!" Rose said, wrapping her wings around him. "Weren't we." She hissed, scowling at Fury.

Fury gave a slight grunt and crept back to the shadows.

"What are you talking about?" Bolt asked, a confused look on his face as his sister backed away from him slightly.

"You were shaking really badly in your sleep and you kept muttering strange things. We tried to wake you up, but you just wouldn't wake up." She said, a tear starting to roll down her snout.

Bolt hated seeing his sister like this. "I'm fine, it was just a nightmare, you don't need to worry about me." Bolt insisted, smiling at his sister and wiping away her tears, trying to calm her down. *At least, I hope it was just a nightmare.* He thought worryingly. *I probably shouldn't tell them what the dream was about, it would only worry them more than they already are.*

Things were beginning to settle down as they started to go back to sleep, when suddenly, they jumped, as a loud roar of terror and pain was heard from outside their cave, coming from the jungle. Rose looked at Bolt with fear in her eyes, and then they rushed towards the cave entrance.

"What was that!?" Rose asked, looking at her brothers.

"I don't know!" Bolt said, panicked, as another piercing shriek came from the jungle. "But I think someone might be in trouble!" he quickly leapt into the sky and darted straight for the jungle.

"Wait!" Rose shouted from behind him, although it was already too late. Bolt was too far out to hear her.

She looked at Fury with a frightened expression. "Aren't you going to go help him!?" she asked, her eyes growing wide with fear.

"No, why would I risk getting myself killed." Fury huffed, going back into the cave, bringing Rose with him.

"But he could die out there!" Rose panicked, trying to get back to the entrance of the cave.

"Then that is his own mistake, there is nothing we can do about it now." Fury snarled, going back into the shadows.

"But we have to try!" Rose shouted, tears starting to build up in her eyes. There was no response from her brother and Rose knew that there was truly nothing she could do. Rose slowly curled up onto the ground, and began to cry.

CHAPTER

2

Bolt flew through the air, his wings getting tired as he began speeding towards the jungle. Even with how sore his wings were getting, he didn't dare slow down. He looked all around, trying to figure out where the scream had come from, all while his mind was becoming a jumbled mess of panicked thoughts.

I can't let them get hurt! But what if something happens to me? I can't leave Rose with my maniac of a brother. His mind spun with fear and worry, his body starting to glow brighter.

There was another deafening roar, and Bolt dove down to where it had come from. When he landed he saw a small dragonet that looked a little like him, but her scales were a bright, silvery white and she didn't have a barb on her tail like him.

Who is that? He thought, trying to figure out what was going on. *I've never seen her here before? What are they doing here?*

The dragonet was bleeding from the several cuts around her body, and she was backed up in front of a large boulder, her eyes wide with fear and pain. She didn't seem to see him though, she was too busy staring at something in front of her. Then Bolt heard a loud hiss and saw what looked like a giant scorpion, closing in on the dragonet, its claws open, stained by blood, and its two tails poised to strike.

What is that!? Bolt thought in a panic. *I've never seen anything like that before! Whatever it is, I can't let it hurt that dragonet! But what am I going to do!? Maybe I can just scare it away?*

Without thinking of an actual plan, Bolt suddenly darted towards the scorpion, ramming into the side of the freakish bug, knocking it a few feet away. The scorpion made a little grunt as it was knocked back. Bolt looked back at the dragonet and saw her staring back at him. She looked at him with a mixed expression of confusion, fear, and joy.

"Look out!" she shouted, pointing to the scorpion with her tail. The scorpion was beginning to shake itself off as it regained its balance, its claws snapping in rage.

"Who dares attack me!?" it let out a loud, insect-like hiss, looking all around. Then all eight of its beady, black, eyes landed right on Bolt. It let out another hiss as its eyes then glanced down and stared directly at the spike that was glowing brightly on Bolt's tail. It seemed to show a small amount of fear before glaring at Bolt. "Impossible!" it snarled. "The royal bloodline is supposed to be dead!" it let out another loud hiss and looked back and forth from Bolt, and the other dragonet, who was still huddled against the rocks.

Royal bloodline? What does it mean by royal bloodline? Surely it can't be talking about me? How could I be royalty, I live in a cave in the middle of nowhere. Bolt thought confused, his mind spinning, trying to think of what he should do next in this situation.

Preparing to attack again, Bolt shook his tail threateningly. It buzzed with energy as he glared at the beast. *Maybe it will leave me alone if I make myself look bigger and more dangerous.* He thought, not breaking eye contact with the scorpion.

"Leave now, or perish!" Bolt hissed, recoiling, and spreading out his wings, trying to make himself look bigger to try and scare the scorpion away, blocking the path between it and the dragonet.

The beast let out a low guttural laugh, which faded into a growl. "Is that so? What are you gonna do? I bet I could kill you in a heartbeat." The scorpion sneered, moving closer to Bolt.

What am I going to do!? Bolt thought in a panic. *I've never had to deal with anything like this before. I might be great at hunting, but I don't know much about fighting, or anything about this creature! What are its strengths? Does it have any weaknesses?* The scorpion took a few more steps, slowly getting closer, opening its claws and preparing to attack. Its claws seemed to dim as they began to turn to stone. They snapped closed with a loud crack as the scorpion continued to move closer.

"I'm going to do whatever I have to do to stop you." Bolt hissed, trying to sound confident. *Please, please believe me. Please just leave so I don't have to fight you.* Bolt thought, panicked.

"Ha! you are no more than a weak dragonet, what could you possibly do?" the scorpion laughed as it continued to close in on the two. "King Scorpious is going to be so glad when he hears I killed a royal thunderfang. Who knows, I might even get a promotion." It sneered, its claws opening again. Bolt looked around, afraid, not knowing what to do.

Don't be afraid. The voice from his dream appeared in his head. *You are stronger than you think. Just let go of your fear and do what you think is right.* The voice said in a calm and soothing tone.

Oh I'm sorry, who's the one currently fighting some kind of freaky mutant scorpion. I don't even know what's right at this point! Bolt thought furiously. *Plus, I've never even been in a fight before... Wait, I think I might have an idea.*

Bolt began piecing together a plan, his tail started glowing brightly, crackling with energy as he prepared to attack. Bolt shook his head, trying to push away the uneasy feelings, right as the scorpion lept at him with a loud hiss, its claws and tails ready to strike.

It felt like time had slowed down, as the scorpion lunged at him. Bolt's mind seemed to go blank and in one quick, fluid motion, Bolt swiftly dodged the attack, and plunged his spiked tail deep into the creature's side, knocking it to the side at the same time. It let out a shriek of pain as it fell over, blackish blood spilling out of its side.

"I tried to warn you." Bolt hissed, snapping his tail like a whip, creating a loud sound like thunder.

"Lucky shot. I've been through worse and now you're really going to pay." It hissed at him, getting back up, ready to strike again. Suddenly one of its stingers shot quickly towards Bolt, trying to inject him with its deadly toxins, but it didn't even manage to make contact. In one fluid motion, Bolt managed to dodge the stinger and slice it off with his tail in one clean slice. The stinger bounced off the ground before skidding to a stop and shriveling up.

The scorpion once again let out a shriek of pain and anger, staring at its missing appendage. What once was a venomous barb was now just a bleeding stump, completely useless.

"What have you done!?" it hissed loudly, glaring at Bolt.

Bolt took this chance and quickly sprung forward, biting into the scorpions side before it could recollect itself. It let out a shriek of fury and pain as Bolt wrapped coil after coil around it, pinning its claws to its side.

"You should have left when you had the chance." Bolt hissed. His throat began to glow even brighter as he unleashed a burst of electricity from his mouth, frying the beast as it screeched and writhed in pain. Without thinking, Bolt continued to fire, blast after blast. He didn't stop until the scorpion had stopped moving, nothing more than a charred exoskeleton.

Realizing what he had just done, he threw the corpse aside with a gasp. He had killed animals before, but nothing like this. He had just killed a giant scorpion that had just tried to kill another dragonet. As he began to catch his breath, he jumped, startled as the dragonet behind him began to speak.

"Thank you for saving me." she said in a soft, heartwarming voice. "I could have died if you hadn't shown up. I'm Sky, I owe you my life." She said, moving close to him, wincing from her wounds.

"I-I'm Bolt." He managed to choke out as he let her rest her head against him. His heart began to speed up as he felt her breath against his scales. *What's going on? Why can't I think straight all of a sudden? I must just be in shock, that's the only reasonable explanation for what's happening.* Bolt thought.

"I couldn't just stay there and let it kill you, so I did what I had to do, you don't owe me anything." Bolt said, his voice shaking.

"Well I'm glad you did. Where did you learn to fight like that anyways?" Sky asked with curiosity and wonder in her eyes.

"I don't know, this is the first fight I've been in. So most of it was me improvising." Bolt responded, still a bit shocked from what had just happened. He just stayed there, still as a statue, unable to move, both from shock, and from a strange new feeling that was starting to spread through him. After a while he remembered that she was badly hurt and quickly turned to face her. "Are you ok? What happened!? Did you get stung!?"

He began spewing out question after question before Sky could finally stop him.

"I'm fine. A little cut up, but overall I'm fine." She winced, forcing a smile.

She's trying to act tough, why? I can clearly see all the blood she's lost. Bolt thought, becoming quite puzzled.

"What was that thing!?" Bolt asked, his voice was still a bit high from the fight.

"You don't already know? That was a dune scorpion. They've been trying to take over this part of the island for years.

"I was sent on a patrol to make sure there was nothing here. Unfortunately for me, there was." She said, wincing in pain.

"Here, let me take you to my cave so I can help you with those cuts. Do you think you can fly right now?" Bolt asked, looking at her wings which had a few cuts in them.

"I don't think so." Sky winced, attempting to take off, only to shrivel back in pain shaking her head.

"It's ok, I think I might be able to carry you on my back and bring you there myself, if that's ok with you." Bolt suggested. Sky gave him a smile and nodded, as he helped her climb up onto his back and he began to fly back to the cave.

Who sends a dragonet on a patrol alone, especially if there are things like that out here!? Bolt thought, looking up at Sky with a worried frown.

As they left, eight glowing beady eyes disappeared into the bushes and the faint sound of scurrying was slowly drowned out by the sounds of the jungle life slowly rising. When they got closer to the cave, Rose came bursting out, flying up to Bolt with a bright and worried smile.

"Where have you been!? We thought you were dead!" she cried as they got inside the cave.

"I'll tell you later, right now there is something more important to worry about." Bolt said. Before he could finish Rose wrapped her wings around Bolt, pulling him into a tight hug, tears rolling down her snout.

"Don't ever leave us again!" she sobbed. Then she looked up and saw the dragonet that Bolt was carrying. "Wait, who's that!?" she asked, looking at the dragonet on Bolts back.

"That's what I wanted to talk about. Her name is Sky and she was attacked by a giant scorpion back in the jungle. I was able to get rid of the scorpion but she still got hurt pretty badly, so I brought her back here." Bolt said, carefully laying Sky down.

"Oh great, another mouth to feed, that's just what we need right now." Fury hissed, coming up to the group.

"Now is not the time for your awful attitude. If you're not going to be helpful then why don't you just back off and stay out of my way!" Bolt snarled at his brother. "Can't you see that she's hurt!" Bolt and Fury went to the back of the cave, snarling and hissing at each other, neither of them noticing that Rose had begun to creep up to Sky.

"Are they always like that?" Sky asked, letting out a small chuckle, before wincing again in pain.

"Yeah, sadly. I'm Rose by the way. It seems you've already met my brother, Bolt. That other one though, the one that Bolt is arguing with is my other brother, Fury. He might act mean and tough but I know he has to have some good in him." Rose responded, moving closer to inspect the wounds.

"I've never seen any of you at the palace before, what are y'all doing out here living in this cave?" Sky asked curiously, before letting out another whimper of pain.

"Here let me help you out with those real quick. I just need you to hold still for a bit" Rose said softly, placing her tail on Sky. Sky gave her a confused look as she watched Rose. The pattern on her tail started to glow a bright pink.

"What are you doing?" Sky said, flinching back a little.

"Don't worry, it is perfectly safe, I just need you to stay still and relax" Rose whispered, placing her tail back on Sky's side. After a while, little branches of strange pink streaks of electricity flowed across her body and covered the wounds, healing them almost instantly. The current flowed around Sky's body, going over any injuries she had.

"How did you do that?" Sky asked with wonder in her voice, looking at where her cuts had once been.

By this time Bolt and Fury had stopped arguing and the two of them also stared at what Rose was doing, completely awestruck.

"More importantly, how long have you been able to do that, and why are we just now finding out." Fury scowled. Bolt jabbed at his side, glaring at him.

"I've never seen anyone do that before." Sky muttered, staring curiously at Rose.

"I don't know how I do it, I just...can. It just started happening a few weeks ago after I tried to go past the jungle and got tangled in a bunch of vines that were covered in thorns. The pattern on my tail just started glowing and all my cuts started disappearing." Rose muttered quietly as she took her tail off Sky.

"You did what!?" Bolt hissed, glaring at his little sister.

"It was only for a second! I wasn't going to go too far!" Rose said quickly. Bolt was about to start fussing at her when he saw that Sky was glaring at him and he decided to back off.

Rose went over to the stream in their cave and washed the blood off of her tail before returning to the group.

"Now you said something about a palace? What palace?" she asked, looking at Sky with a confused expression. She then looked up at her brothers and noticed that Bolt had winced when she asked the question. "What's wrong? Is there something you want to tell us?" she asked, concerned.

"Well... there actually is something I need to tell you, something that I've been worrying about ever since last night." Bolt admitted, his eyes widening with fear. "I had a dream last night, some sort of vision I think. There was this voice, and it mentioned something about a palace.

"It told me that if we didn't leave this cave, bad things would happen, very bad things, and not only to us, but to anyone who is at that palace."

"Wait, did you say visions?" Sky asked, her voice growing serious. "When did you start having these visions?"

"Last night, why?" Bolt asked, suddenly a little bit curious about why Sky was interested in this.

"Hmm, that's...strange." Sky muttered quietly, without answering Bolts question.

"Wait, but I thought you said that we weren't ready to leave the cave?" Rose interjected, with fear in her eyes.

"I'm perfectly ready. I could have left whenever I wanted to." Fury snarled. "You're the ones that are scared of everything." The two ignored Furys negative words.

"I don't think we have a choice anymore." Bolt said warmly to his sister, trying to calm her down. "Don't worry, wherever we are, just know that I will always be there to protect you." He said, lifting her chin with his tail. Rose smiled and nodded her head in agreement before looking at Fury and then back at Bolt. "I have a feeling we need to start by finding the palace." Bolt said, looking at his brother and sister.

"I'm coming too." Sky announced, getting up with a fierce look in her eyes.

"What!? You can't come! You were just attacked! You need time to recover." Bolt said quickly, shaking his head.

"Oh well, then I guess you're going to have to find another way to get to the palace." Sky said, letting out a fake sigh and beginning to lay back down.

"Ugh, fine, you're right, you can come with us." Bolt groaned in aggravation. Sky got up as quick as she could and gave Bolt a little teasing smirk. "Well when are we going?"

CHAPTER

3

"Are we there yet?" Rose whined as they stopped to rest after a long day of traveling.

"We should be there soon." Sky replied.

"I think you don't even know where you're going!" Fury snarled impatiently.

"Is it too hard for you to stop complaining for at least five minutes!" Bolt let out a low hiss, glaring at his brother. "I'm sure Sky knows where she's going." He added, quickly flying up to Sky. "You do know where you're going, right?" he asked quietly, looking at her with a nervous smile.

"Yes Bolt, I do, you don't have to worry all the time." She said, letting out a little laugh. "You can't live by being worried about everything. Trust me, I know." Bolt wanted to point out that the reason they have lived so long is because he had been worrying about everything, not because he was a coward, but because he wanted to keep everyone safe.

"Do you think we could at least stop and rest for today? My wings hurt from flying all day." Rose whined, slowing down, completely out of breath.

Sky looked around and saw how tired everyone looked. She didn't want to admit it, but she was feeling really tired as well.

"Fine, I don't see why we can't take a break for the night. We'll make a little shelter to sleep in for tonight and we'll leave first thing in the morning." Everyone let out a sigh of relief, glad to finally be able to take a break.

After finding a good spot to land, the four of them decided to split apart the work. Fury and Rose started looking for the materials to create their temporary shelter, while Bolt and Sky went out to start gathering other supplies for the night. Bolt had also decided that he would go out by himself later, to take a quick survey around the area and make sure the area was safe for them, before eventually heading back to the group. When he got back to their shelter he saw that Sky had started helping Rose build a little tent for them to sleep in.

"Nice job with the tent." He said, going up to them to help with the finishing touches, smiling when he saw the happy expression on his sister's face. When they finished, they took a few minutes to relax. Bolt looked around for his brother but didn't see him anywhere.

"Where's Fury?" he asked, looking at Sky and Rose.

"He went off on his own somewhere, he didn't tell us where he was going, but I'm sure he will come back, probably." Rose replied, giving Bolt a worried smile. Then Bolt's stomach made a low growl and he realized he hadn't eaten anything since the night they had left.

"Hey I'm going to go get us something to eat. Do y'all want anything specific or are you ok with whatever I can find?" he said, starting to turn around.

"Great! I'll come too." Sky said, moving quickly beside him.

"I would prefer to hunt alone. I find it a lot easier when I don't have to worry about anyone else scaring off any prey. Anyways you should stay here, where it's safe." He said, trying to keep a stern look on his face as she moved up beside him.

"Oh don't be such a worry wart, I'll be fine." She laughed. "I could use some exercise anyways and what better way to do that than to go hunting. And I promise I won't scare off any of your precious prey." She added, teasing him. Bolt stopped and hesitated before finally speaking.

"Fine you can come along, but please try not to get into any more trouble. I might not be there to save you next time."

"I just think you're just nervous around her because you like her." Rose teased, letting out a little giggle.

"What! No! I don't like her. I mean, I don't not like her. She's a good friend, that's all!" Bolt said quickly, starting to blush.

"Mhm." Rose smirked. "Well you know what I want." She said, heading back to the little shelter they had made.

"Let me guess. You want the biggest goat I can find." Bolt smirked, teasing her. "Alright, alright, I'll see what kind of fruit I can find." He chuckled, glad to have changed the topic. Sky gave him a confused look when he said that. "Oh yeah, Rose doesn't like meat. She really likes animals, so she tends to stick to eating fruit most of the time." Bolt explained, seeing Skys confused expression.

"Huh," She muttered, "I've only met a few dragons who do that. She doesn't eat any kind of meat?"

"Nope, not if she doesn't have too." Bolt replied.

The two of them went into the jungle to hunt. They picked up the scent of a few monkeys that had been around the area. They followed the scent until they came up to a small group of monkeys, and hid in the brush, waiting for the right moment to attack.

"So...what's with your brother? Has he always been so grumpy and mean?" Sky whispered quietly, breaking the silence.

"It's not something I like to talk about." Bolt said, trying to keep his voice down, his eyes locked onto the monkeys. *Welp there goes the chance of having a normal hunting trip. Maybe if I act like I wasn't paying attention she won't ask any more questions.* Bolt thought, slightly annoyed. "Now, I want you to do exactly what I do." He said quickly, as he began to slowly creep up closer to the monkeys. Sky gave him a little frown, but followed what he did anyways and soon they were close enough to be in striking distance.

"It might just be me, but I feel like you're avoiding the question." Sky whispered, glancing at Bolt.

Why does she want to know about my brother so badly? Bolt thought, annoyed at her persistence. "Ok now we're going to rush at them on the count of three. If we are lucky we might get more than one each." He whispered, still ignoring her question. "One...two...three!" Bolt burst out of the brush, lunging at the small group and snatching a monkey in his jaws, killing it instantly.

Sky quickly did the same but was a little off target and she slammed into the tree that the monkeys were hanging on.

She did manage to grab two monkeys from the group before they ran away.

"You ok?" Bolt laughed, helping her up. "I probably should have been more specific and said you want to catch them in your mouth." Sky gave him a gentle shove before bursting into laughter as well. As they sat there laughing, the jungle seemed to grow quiet before Sky finally decided to break the silence.

"You can tell me anything, you do know that, right? Whatever it is, I promise I will only take it seriously." she asked with a hopeful and heart warming smile, looking Bolt in the eyes.

Am I really going to tell her about us? I mean, what if she tells anyone else. She wouldn't do that, not after all we've done for her. Maybe it's time for me to start trusting others and let down my guard. Bolt thought, looking at Sky.

"Fury wasn't always like that." Bolt admitted finally, letting out a defeated sigh. "After he hatched, he was actually a lot like Rose, easily excited and willing to do anything. But over time he began to grow bitter. He started avoiding us and arguing with us. Then he just stopped talking to us period, he would just stay in the dark corners of our cave for hours upon hours.

"I worry about him sometimes. He may not be the best dragon out there, but he's still family. And I just want him to go back to being his old self." He said, trying to hold back tears.

"Oh." Sky said quietly with a frown, looking at Bolt. "I'm sorry. I wouldn't have asked if I knew it was so personal." She added with a warm smile, wrapping her tail around his, trying to cheer him up.

"No no, it's fine, I'm glad you did anyways." Bolt smiled, looking into her eyes as time seemed to slow.

"We should probably get back before the others start to worry." Sky said quickly, her face quickly turning red.

"Wait! We still need to get something for Rose." Bolt said to remind her, but then stopped as he saw Sky holding a bushel of bananas. "How did you-?" he started before getting cut off.

"You're not the only quick one here, are you?" she smirked with a look of triumph on her face. "I found a few banana trees on our way over here so I decided to grab some for Rose."

"That's great! Do you think we should get something for my brother just in case?" Bolt asked, grabbing the monkeys.

"I think that lump on a log should go hunt for himself. He needs to learn that if he isn't going to be nice, he isn't going to get anything in return from us." She snorted, shaking her head. Then she picked up the bananas and started heading back.

When the two of them got back to their shelter, Rose was there waiting for them, her tail shaking with excitement when she saw them.

"So how did things go?" Rose teased, looking at the two of them, their tails still intertwined.

"Fine! Everything went fine." Bolt said quickly, unwinding his tail. "Where's Fury?"

"Oh, he's already asleep. He had caught himself a few lizards while you were out hunting." Rose replied with a smile.

"Good. Because we didn't get him anything." Sky said as she put down the bananas.

"Ooo, bananas! I haven't had those in forever!" Rose squealed as Sky broke off a few of the bananas and passed them to her.

Then Rose looked up at something that was moving on Skys back and let out an excited squeal, "You've got something cute and fuzzy on your back!" she rushed over and grabbed the little monkey that had managed to climb onto Skys back. "I think I'll name you...Tiny." She smiled, holding the monkey up and letting it climb onto her back.

"I don't think it's a good idea to give it a name. You don't want to get too attached, in case something happens to it." Bolt said scornfully.

"Well I'm not going to let anything happen to him. Isn't that right Tiny?" Rose said playfully to the monkey, before heading into the little shelter.

"Didn't I just...oh nevermind." Bolt said sourly, as he started to eat.

"I think it would be very kind of you to let her keep it. She seemed pretty happy when she saw it." Sky said, moving beside him. She began to eat her share and the two of them stayed out there for a while, just looking up into the night sky. "Do you see those stars?" she asked, pointing at a group of stars that were shining brighter than the rest.

"Yes, what about them?" Bolt asked curiously, looking at the stars and then back at her.

"Some say those are the spirits of previous kings. The better the king, the brighter the star." she said, leaning against him. "Do you see that really bright one?" she asked, pointing to the star in the middle.

"Yes." Bolt said, his heart beginning to beat faster when he felt her lean against his side.

"That's from our last king, King Whirlwind. He was one of the greatest kings of our entire tribe. He saved our entire tribe from being ruled by a wicked queen. It is also said that if you listen carefully, you can hear the voices of their spirits speaking to you." She said with a dreamy look on her face.

"Is that so?" Bolt asked, his mind going back to the voice from his dreams.

"Yeah. I've always wanted to hear them speak, but they never do." She sighed and let out a loud yawn.

"I think it's time we got some sleep." Bolt smiled, also letting out a yawn as he went into the shelter. Shortly after, he felt her curl up beside him.

"Goodnight Bolt." She yawned, her voice already getting quieter from exhaustion.

"Goodnight Sky." He smiled back at her as she closed her eyes. Soon he could hear her breath soften as she began to fall asleep. Bolt laid his head down and closed his eyes and thought to himself. *Is that the voice I've been hearing in my head? Was that a spirit trying to talk with me? If so, who?* He slowly began to drift away into sleep, the only thing he felt was the calm atmosphere around him.

"You made the right decision, I'm very proud of you." The voice said in his head.

Bolt slowly opened his eyes and found himself in that same endless darkness from before. "So you are real..." Bolt said slowly.

"I am very much real." The voice said softly. "Not as real as I once was, but real nonetheless."

"Are you a spirit?" Bolt asked with a hopeful and curious expression. He looked around trying to locate where the voice was coming from but saw nothing except darkness on all sides.

"Yes I am indeed a spirit." The voice said calmly. "Everything that your friend said was true."

"Then who are you?" Bolt asked, the curiosity in his voice rising. "And why can't I see you?"

"Because I have yet to show myself to you." The voice responded after a moment of silence.

"Why not? I would find it quite helpful to know who I'm speaking with." Bolt said, slightly annoyed.

"Do you really wish to know?" the voice asked, its calming tone slightly masking its uneasiness.

"Yes, I do. I want to know who you are." Bolt said. Slowly the darkness began to fade away and a little field began to form.

"Very well then, if that is truly what you want." The voice said before fading away for a moment. All of a sudden a dragon slowly began to form in front of Bolt. This dragon was quite larger than Bolt, but looked very similar, except for the pattern along their side. "Hello Bolt, I am King Whirlwind. I go by many names but you can call me dad."

CHAPTER

4

"Dad!?" Bolt repeated, shocked and confused, unable to process what was going on.

"That's right! You are the son of the greatest king in our tribe's history. Not to brag or anything." Whirlwind said with a small chuckle, looking down at Bolt.

"So that's why the dune scorpion said I was part of the royal bloodline." Bolt said, amazed and still, a bit confused. "Wait, how was he able to tell?" he asked, confused.

"You see that spike on your tail?" Whirlwind said with a smile. "Only the royal family have those." He twisted his tail showing the large spike.

"So that's why Sky didn't have one." Bolt said, amazed, looking at the spike on his fathers tail.

"Yep. By the way, I think you and Sky are going to make a great team." His father said, winking at him.

"What! No! It's not like that!" Bolt said, feeling himself starting to blush.

"That's exactly what I thought at first when I met your mother." His father said, before letting out a sigh. An image of another dragon began to form beside them and Bolt assumed it was his mother.

"Woah is that her?" Bolt asked, looking at the image. He noticed that she didn't look like him or his father. She was a light blue, like the color of ice, her underscales glowing a darker blue.

"Her name was Snowstorm. She was born with a rare defect that affected her scales and gave her the power to breath out a freezing cloud." Whirlwind said with a small smile. "She was the love of my life. Until she betrayed me to try and take the throne for herself!" he said with a hiss.

"Is that how you died? Were you killed by her?" Bolt asked curiously, slowly starting to get angry.

"Not exactly. She was one of the reasons, but I died using an artifact to seal her away. The power was too much for me and it killed me in the process." His father sighed.

"Is that why you wanted us to go to the palace? Because of her?" Bolt asked, looking up at his father. "So what I saw was real, is that what's going to happen?"

"It is one possibility, yes. But there are other things that could happen." His father said, as the fields started morphing and changing, taking the appearance of the same large palace, completely intact, with dragons all around. Then Bolt saw Sky, except she looked much older, around the same age as his father. He thought he saw her say something, and soon after that, three dragonets that looked a little younger than Bolt came up to her.

"Who's dragonets are those? Why are they crowding around Sky?" Bolt asked, looking up at his father

"Well they are only crowding around her because you were quite busy somewhere else." Whirlwind said with a smile, looking down at Bolt. Bolt paused for a moment and then gasped as he realized what his father ment.

"Are you trying to tell me that those are-?" Bolt started.

"Your dragonets, yes, they are." his father said, looking at Bolt with a smile. "This is what your life could look like if you manage to save our kingdom." Bolt continued to watch the hyper dragonets fly around Sky in little circles, his face lighting up with hope and joy.

So this is what I can expect if everything goes right. But, what if seeing this means it will never happen now? Bolt thought. He looked back towards the palace and smiled as he saw his sister come up to them and the three dragonets sped toward her with big smiles.

Bolt laughed when he saw this, but then something completely unexpected happened. He saw his brother come up beside them with another dragon with him. Their tails were wrapped around each other, and they kept looking at each other.

Who is that? Why is Fury with them? I thought Fury hated being around us. Bolt thought, a puzzled frown spread across his face.

He tried to see who this strange dragon was, but before he could get a good look at them, everything suddenly vanished.

His eyes slowly opened as the morning light shined down on his face.

"Good morning sleepy head." Sky smiled, entering the little shelter. "You woke up just in time for breakfast." She said, passing him a large mango.

"Thank you." Bolt said, taking the mango and taking a large bite out of it.

"So did you have any good dreams last night?" Sky asked, giving Bolt a small smile. Bolt stopped for a moment before answering her question.

"Unfortunately no, just another dreamless sleep." Bolt sighed, trying to sound convincing. *I don't think it is a good idea to tell her what I actually saw.* Bolt thought as he took another bite of the mango. He had tried to make it look like he enjoyed it so he wouldn't hurt her feelings.

"You don't like it, do you?" she snickered, seeing the expression on his face. "I wasn't a big fan of mine either."

"Rose put you up to this, didn't she?" Bolt said with a smile, happy that the subject had changed. "Who am I kidding of course she did."

Bolt let out a yawn and slowly got out of the shelter they had made and looked around. He saw that everyone was already getting ready to continue their journey.

"If we go now we should get to the palace by noon." Sky said with a hint of excitement in her voice.

"I can't believe we're going to see a real life palace!" Rose squealed, almost shaking Tiny off of her back.

"At least someone was smart enough to get a snack for the flight." Fury said sourly, glaring at the little monkey.

"Tiny is not food!" Rose hissed, glaring at Fury. "And don't even think about trying to take him!"

"Whatever." He said with a snort, rolling his eyes. Soon the group started flying again, following Sky. After a while Bolt decided to fly next to her. He still had the image of them from the dream and he had a big smile on his face. *If what my father showed me was true, then maybe me and Sky could be happy, and who knows, we might even find the dragonet I saw with Fury. I just wish I could get a better look at them.* Bolt thought to himself, before his thoughts were interrupted by Sky.

"You seem awfully happy." Sky laughed, as Bolt did a little loop in the air. "What's on your mind?"

"Oh nothing, just in a good mood." He said quickly. *I can't tell her what I saw, what if it changes how things end.* Bolt thought to himself.

"I think I know what's on his mind, and I bet it's more like who's on his mind." Rose teased, flying up beside them, giving Bolt a silly smile.

"You're really not going to give that up are you?" Bolt asked with a sigh.

"Nope!" she said gleefully, doing a little twirl in the air.

"So Sky, what's the palace like anyways?" Bolt asked, looking at Sky with a curious expression, trying to do anything to change the subject.

"Oh it's great!" Sky said excitedly. "It's really big and the dragons there are very nice. Well, most of them at least. I'm sure you'll love it there."

"Do you really think so?" Bolt asked her, giving her a little smile. *Wow, she makes it sound so perfect. I just hope that it actually ends up being that way.* Bolt thought.

"Yep" Sky replied, giving him a small smile back. The two of them continued talking as they flew, with Sky getting more and more excited the longer they talked about the kingdom.

"Are you two lovebirds done? I do believe that you're supposed to be taking us to a palace and I have yet to see that happen. All you've done so far is have us fly to some random mountain range while talking to Bolt like you were a married couple." Fury hissed from behind them, beginning to grow impatient.

"We're here!" Sky shouted with excitement, ignoring Furys comment. She dived down to a cave that was near the base of one of the mountains and ducked inside. Then she poked her head out and looked at the others. "You guys coming?"

Bolt looked at the others, confused, shrugged, and then dived down to follow Sky. He entered the cave and was immediately hit with another wave of confusion.

Surely this can't be it, right? This just looks like any ordinary cave to me. Bolt thought to himself. He looked around, trying to spot anything that might be out of the ordinary.

"I knew you didn't know where you were going! You just took us to another cave!" Fury hissed, his tail lashing back and forth, buzzing with energy.

"Is this it? It doesn't look like much." Rose asked, confused, looking at the cave. "I'd imagined it would have been a lot bigger." She said with a frown.

"Oh no this isn't the palace. This is just the entrance to our kingdom, watch." Sky smiled, her eyes filled with joy and excitement. She went over to the far wall in the back of the cave and stopped. Bolt could see that there was a little crack in the wall. Sky leaned in closer to the little crack. Then she shot out a small burst of electricity into the crack. Bolt's jaw dropped as he gasped, seeing the energy travel through the crack, seeming to stretch out and take the shape of a small doorway. Sky looked back at him with a smile.

"Cool right?" Sky snickered, looking back towards the wall. Then a little rumble could be felt as the ground began to shake, the cracks along the wall starting to grow, as the wall in front of them opened up.

"Welcome to the thunderfang kingdom!" Sky said excitedly, as she went through the doorway. The others followed and saw what looked to be a town with a massive structure in the middle. But what really amazed them is that when they entered it looked as if the top of the mountain had vanished, the sun shining down on the town.

"Wow!" Rose gasped, her eyes filled with wonder as she looked around, seeing several dragons flying in the sky. "This place is beautiful!"

"How is this possible?" Bolt asked, amazed, looking up at where the mountain top should have been.

"One of our kings used magic to create this mountain during the great war to keep us hidden and safe. When you enter through that doorway the top of the mountain vanishes, but only from the inside. From the outside it still just looks like a regular mountain." Sky said with a large smile. She took a deep breath and let out a sigh. "It feels so good to finally be back home." She smiled.

"Who goes there?" a voice demanded, as three dragons came up to them, with their tails wrapped around what looked like spears. But these spears had what looked like a glowing spike on the top, just like the spike on Bolt's tail.

"It's just me, Sky. And guess what? You'll never believe who I found while I was out scouting!" Sky said excitedly.

"Ugh, not again, what have you brought back home this time?" the guard sighed, shaking his head. "And who are these three? I've never seen them around here before?"

"Oh, um, this is Bolt." Sky smiled, wrapping her tail around Bolt's with a big smile. "The pink one is Rose, and the really grumpy one right over there is Fury. And guess what! They're Whirlwinds missing dragonets!"

The guard looked skeptically at the group. He didn't seem to believe Sky and started muttering to himself, looking at the other guards.

Show him your tail. Whirlwind's voice said in Bolt's head.

Oh right! Bolt thought. He raised his tail, showing the glowing spike on it. The guards took one look at it and gasped.

"It really is them!" one of them whispered, staring at Bolt's tail.

"But I thought Whirlwind's eggs were destroyed?" another whispered back.

"Quiet, both of you! My apologies, your highness. We all thought the royal bloodline had died out a long time ago. Please, come in, everyone is going to be so happy when they hear about this." The third guard apologized, giving them a little bow.

I can't believe this. Bolt thought. *All my life I thought I was normal. Yet here I am, a prince! I'm finally where I was meant to be.*

"Please, let us show you around, my name's Cyclone." The guard said and turned around, shouting a few orders at the other guards. Then he flew off in the direction of the town and motioned for them to follow. "This is the town that surrounds the palace." He said, gesturing to the rows of buildings as they flew by them. "Our kingdom is split up into three different groups. The scouts, which reside in the lower section of the town.

"The hunters, which reside near the middle section of the town.

"And the guards, which reside in the upper section of the town." He turned to them, giving them a big smile. "And you, the royal family, will be staying in that large building in the center of the town." He pointed at the large structure that was giving off a slight glow.

"This place is so cool!" Rose squealed in excitement, her entire body shaking. Tiny had to cling tighter around her to keep from getting flung off.

"I think this place is far too bright." Fury muttered, moving away from his sister. When he did this he bumped into another dragonet that looked to be about the same age as him.

"Oh, I am so, so sorry! I'm such a klutz! I should probably just get going now." She said quickly, trying to avoid eye contact. Bolt looked at Fury, worried about how he would react to this.

Please don't do anything irrational. He thought worryingly. But surprisingly, when he looked at Furys face, he swore he could see his expression soften for just a second before Fury saw Bolt staring at him.

"What are you looking at?" he hissed at Bolt, before turning back to face the dragonet.

"Oh don't mind her. she's a nobody after all, wasn't even born in the kingdom. She is what we call an outsider." Cyclone sighed, rolling his eyes.

"You do know we were born outside of the kingdom, right?" Rose pointed out, giving the guard an annoyed expression.

"Oh, uh, but that's ok, since you're royals." Cyclone said quickly, giving her an apologetic look before turning back around.

"So what's your name?" Fury hissed at the dragonet, seeming to burn a hole in her head with his glare.

"Rainstorm." She muttered nervously, not being able to look away from his eyes, too scared to move.

"Well then, Rainstorm, I'm Fury. And normally I would have severely punished someone for doing what you just did, but I'm going to pretend it never happened because I'm in a good mood right now." He snarled, looking away from her.

Good mood? Bolt thought, confused. *I've never heard him say that before.* He looked at Rainstorm and the dragonet from his dream appeared in his head. An idea slowly started forming in his head. *Maybe this is the dragonet from my dream that was with Fury. I might not be able to save the entire kingdom, but I can at least try to give my brother a happy ending.* He thought. "So, Rainstorm, would you like to come with us?" Bolt asked, giving her a big grin. All of a sudden everyone started staring at him with the same confused expression. Everyone, except for Fury, who just glared at him.

"I-I don't think that's a good idea." Rainstorm stuttered nervously. She was shaking slightly with stress and embarrassment.

"I really don't think the future king should be talking to a low life like her." Cyclone said scornfully, glaring at Rainstorm. Fury shuttered when Cyclone referred to Bolt as a king. He glared at his brother, the spike on his tail starting to glow and buzz with energy.

"What's wrong with that?" Rose hissed, glaring at the Cyclone. "I say she can come." She said, her spiked tail starting to glow. Rainstorm smiled when she heard Rose standing up for her.

"Well I guess I can come." Rainstorm muttered, trying to act confident. Bolt smiled, looking at her.

"Well then, welcome to the team!"

CHAPTER

5

"What are you up to?" Sky whispered to Bolt as they were brought into the palace. Cyclone had just finished showing them around the town and had stopped at the palace doors.

"Nothing!" Bolt said quickly. Sky saw through his lie and gave him a stern glare.

"Don't lie to me." she hissed. "I know you're up to something."

"Alright everyone, I have to get back to my post, so unfortunately I will not be able to show you around the palace." Cyclone said, before Bolt could respond to Sky, looking at the group. "Stormcloud, get over here right now!" he shouted.

"Coming!" a voice shouted from a distance. A solid gray dragonet with bright yellow underscales came zooming across the palace before stopping directly in front of Cyclone. The dragonet looked just a bit younger than Bolt, by maybe a year or two. The dragonet looked up at Cyclone with a serious expression. "What is it dad?" the dragonet asked, before looking at the group.

"This is my son, Stormcloud. He will be showing you around the palace for now. Feel free to ask him anything." Cyclone said, before flying out of the room. Stormcloud turned to the group and smiled at them.

"So you three must be Whirlwind's missing dragonets, it's an honor to meet you in person." He said, giving them a little bow. "Now for the other two of you, you would be?" He looked up with a confused expression.

"Oh I'm Sky. I'm the one that found them! Isn't that great!?" Sky said excitedly. "And she's Rainstorm. She's a bit shy from what I know." Sky said, putting a wing around Rainstorm, who was trying desperately to avoid eye contact. Stormcloud eyed the two before looking back at Bolt, Fury, and Rose.

"I can't believe I get the honor of speaking to the last remaining dragons of the royal bloodline!" He said with a smile, staring directly at Bolt.

Wow, everyone seems so excited about us, we can't really be that special, can we? Bolt thought, looking long and hard at Stormcloud.

"As my father said, my name's Stormcloud, but I prefer to just be called Storm, it makes it a little less of a mouthful. Now if you would all follow me, I'll show you around the palace and where you will be staying." Storm announced, looking at the group. He went down one of the hallways and gestured for the group to follow him.

"Isn't he just the coolest?" Rose asked, with a dreamy look on her face. "I wonder if he likes monkeys?" she muttered quietly to herself. Bolt looked at his sister with a confused expression.

"I mean I guess he's alright? He definitely seems pretty nice." Bolt replied, quite confused about what she was talking about before seeing the dazed look on her face.

"Ohh, I see what's going on. I think someone has a little crush, don't you agree?" He smirked.

"W-what! No you don't! I do not! Stop looking at me!" Rose responded quickly, frantically trying to hide her face with her wings as she began to blush.

"Who's the one going all googly eyed over another dragon now?" Bolt smirked, giving her a teasing grin.

"Wait, so you're admitting to liking Sky?" Rose remarked, looking back up at him.

"What! No! That is not what I said!" Bolt said quickly. "Hey we should probably catch up with the others before they get too far ahead!" he added, trying to change the topic to anything other than this. He quickly rushed over to the group with Rose following close behind him.

"And to the right you will see the royal kitchen where almost anything can be made there." Storm announced, pausing as the two made their way back into the group.

"What were you two doing back there?" Sky asked, puzzled, looking at Bolt right in the eyes with a bit of suspicion.

"Just talking with Rose." Bolt replied quickly, looking away to avoid her stare. "Nothing to worry about."

"Now unfortunately, we will have to continue the tour tomorrow because it is getting quite late. Sky, Rainstorm, time for you to head back to your living quarters." Storm said, looking at both Sky and Rainstorm.

"O-ok." Rainstorm muttered quietly. She quickly turned around and started heading toward the exit.

"Wait! Rainstorm, come back." Bolt shouted quickly. She looked back at him with a confused expression as she slowly began to return to the group. "I wouldn't mind it if both you and Sky stayed here for tonight. If you're ok with staying of course?" he insisted, glancing at Storm.

"It's fine with me if they stay, you're the one that's basically in charge anyways." Storm added, giving them a little shrug.

"Great! Then Sky can stay with me and Rose. Which means Rainstorm will be staying with Fury." Bolt said as Sky smiled at him.

"W-What!" Rainstorm stammered nervously, glancing at Fury, who was currently fuming, glaring at his brother with pure hatred. "You want me to stay with him!? I really don't think that's a good idea." She stammered.

"What makes you think I want to stay with her?" Fury hissed, glaring at Bolt. He paused when he saw how hurt Rainstorm looked when he had said that.

"It's just one night. I think you two could become great friends." Bolt insisted confidently, trying to hold back a smile.

"Don't get used to bossing us around like this. You're not the only prince around here, I could end up being king just as much as you!" Fury hissed, his scales beginning to glow a faint red.

"Ok then, Fury, Rainstorm, follow me and I will take you to your room." Storm replied, going down a separate hallway. He led Fury and Rainstorm to one of the rooms on the right and brought the others to another room on the right which was larger than the others.

Please don't act out Fury. I'm just trying to help you. Bolt thought as he entered the room. He paused when he saw a few small, circular pools of water, just a few inches deep, decorating with shining gems and other treasures. Each one had four glowing crystals fixed into the side of the pools.

"What are those?" Bolt asked, confused, looking down at the strange pools, poking at one of the glittering gems with his tail.

"Oh yeah I forgot to tell you, We have to sleep in these shallow pools of water, which we call static pools, to regain the energy we lost whenever we use our powers." Sky responded, giving him a small example by breathing out a small streak of electricity as white as a shining star.

Snap out of it Bolt, you don't have time for things like this! Bolt thought, shaking his head, trying to rid himself of the image of him and Sky from his vision. He looked back at Sky as she brought him and Rose to one of the pools. "When we sleep, we let out an electric charge from our bodies and when we are in the pools, that electricity flows around in the water, reflecting off of the crystals along the edges, which gets reabsorbed into our body, helping us regain that missing energy.

"When we lose too much energy we get weaker, and if we lose all of our energy we die." Sky added, stopping when she saw their nervous expressions.

"But, we haven't been sleeping in pools like this. Why didn't we die?" Rose asked, confused.

"It's probably because we didn't really use our electricity back in our cave, but now that I think of it I've been feeling a little bit tired ever since that fight I had with the dune scorpion." Bolt muttered, trying to get a closer look at the pools. "And you're absolutely sure they're safe?" he asked cautiously.

"Yep! Absolutely safe. You really do need to stop worrying so much about everything. Not everything is out to get you." Sky replied, smiling at Bolt.

"Well as long as you're sure that they're safe. Rose why don't you-" Bolt started, before looking at Rose, who was already fast asleep in one of the pools. A glowing pinkish current was moving around in the water in little streaks as she started to glow a faint pink. Tiny was asleep by the side of the pool in a little bed Rose had managed to make for him when Bolt and Sky had been talking. Bolt smiled and looked back at Sky and saw that she was staring at him with a scowl on her face.

"What?" Bolt asked, looking at her confused, letting out a nervous chuckle.

"You know exactly what." She responded with a slight hiss. "You're up to something. Now spill!"

"I'm not up to anything! I promise!" Bolt said quickly, trying to make it sound believable.

"I thought we were friends." She sighed, a frown forming across her face. "And friends don't lie to each other." She sighed again, shaking her head and slowly started moving over to another pool. Bolt's heart seemed to stop after she had said that.

"Wait! Just, wait." Bolt sighed in defeat, coming over to her. "Are you sure you really want to know?"

"Yes, I would like to know what you're planning so I can try to stop you in case it's a bad idea." She replied with a triumphant smile.

I don't think I can lie my way out of this one. Well then, here goes nothing. Bolt thought before moving beside her. "I had another weird vision last night. It was very different from the first one. We were much older and living in the palace with my brother and sister.

"But what really stood out to me was that Fury had another dragon with him, and it looked like they enjoyed each others company. I didn't get a really good look at her, but I swear she looked just like Rainstorm." Bolt confessed. *I still think I shouldn't tell her about my father though. That could cause her to start worrying about me.* He thought, looking at Sky.

"Are you sure that's all?" she asked, wrapping her tail around his. Bolt nodded and she stared at him for a long time before giving him a big hug.

"I'm glad you finally told me the truth." She smiled, letting go of him.

"Yeah...The truth..." Bolt muttered quietly as he moved to one of the bigger pools. He looked down at his reflection and sighed before getting in.

The water was cold at first, but he eventually got used to it. He curled up in the water and laid his head down, going deep into thought.

I really hope I didn't make a mistake. I hope Rainstorm is alright and that my brother isn't making her feel bad about herself. He thought to himself before closing his eyes. As he slowly drifted asleep he began to remember the dream that he had last night and began to think about that mysterious dragon that was with his brother.

Yes. Everything is going to be fine. Sky is right, there is no reason for me to worry. He thought before finally falling asleep. All of a sudden Bolt felt like he was hovering in the air. He slowly opened his eyes and once again, he saw the empty void that had been haunting his dreams the last couple of nights.

Except this time there seemed to be one single light seeming to come from above him, but when Bolt looked up he saw nothing up there that could have been creating the strange light. The light seemed to be shining down on a single glowing pedestal. On that pedestal, Bolt saw what looked like a strange obsidian amulet with five different colored gems fused into it. The amulet seemed to have been surrounded by a thick box of glass which reflected the light that was shining down on it.

What is that? Bolt thought as he crept up closer to the pedestal, staring at the gems that had begun to glow faintly.

"Dad? Are you doing this? Are you here?" He shouted out into the darkness. There was no response.

Open the case. Bolt was startled, as a new voice began to speak. This voice was raspy and always shifting, with a slight buzz that echoed each time it spoke.

"Who's there!?" Bolt jumped, hearing this strange new voice.

Open the case. The strange voice repeated again, louder.

"Dad, if this is some kind of trick, it's not funny! I would really like it if you would please stop!" Bolt shouted frantically, looking around, trying to pinpoint the location of this strange new voice.

Open the case! The voice repeated even louder this time. Then a loud screeching could be heard that seemed to be coming from every direction. *Open the case! Open the case! OPEN, THE, CASE!* It repeated faster and faster. Finally it got to the point where Bolt couldn't handle anymore of the shouting and screeching.

"Alright! Alright! I'll open the case!" Bolt shouted, whipping his tail, creating another thunderous crack. Then all at once both the voice and the screeching silenced as Bolt slowly began to remove the glass case. "There is absolutely no reason for all that noise." Bolt muttered sourly, looking closely at the amulet. He reached his tail out to grab the amulet, and no sooner had he touched it did a searing pain begin to quickly spread across his body. Then everything vanished, as he was forced out of the dream. When he opened his eyes he found Tiny sitting on his snout, as Rose was staring at him with the same worried look from before, this time with Sky beside her, her face also showing large amounts of panic.

"I did it again, didn't I?" Bolt sighed, lifting his head as Tiny jumped off onto Rose. Rose nodded and Sky helped him out of the pool.

"Was it another nightmare?" his sister asked, looking at him with worried eyes.

"I'm not sure. This felt so real. And it felt like I was forced out of it by some kind of unseen force." Bolt stammered, his voice shaking. His entire body was shaking from what had just happened. Sky wrapped her wings around him, pulling him into another hug.

"I'm just glad you're ok. I thought you had some sort of bad reaction from being in the pool for the first time." She replied, tears beginning to fall down her face. "This is all my fault!"

"No! This isn't your fault. I don't think I had that dream because of the pool. It felt like something was calling to me from outside my dream, something in this palace.

"The only thing I saw was a strange amulet on a pedestal. When I touched it I was forced out of my own dream." Bolt whispered to her, trying to calm her down. He wiped away her tears and looked her in the eyes. Time once again began to slow, before Fury suddenly burst into the room with a snarl.

"Come on, everyone get up, Storm wants us ready so he can finish showing us around." Fury hissed, glaring at the three. "Rainstorm and I are already up and I would like to get this over with as soon as possible."

CHAPTER

6

"Good morning." Storm said, smiling at the three of them as they came out of their room. "Glad to see you'll finally be joining us for the rest of the tour."

"Aren't we going to eat first?" Bolt asked, looking at Storm and letting out a loud yawn.

"Yeah I'm starving!" Rose added with excitement when she saw Storm. She then started rapidly asking Storm question after question. "Do you have any fruit? You do eat fruit here right? I wouldn't be seeming weird because I like fruit, right?" Storm went quiet, a bit confused by all the questions she was asking, before finally starting to speak.

"No, you wouldn't seem weird for liking fruit. In fact we have quite a wide variety of fruits and vegetables that are grown all around the kingdom. But we can eat later, right now I would like to finish up the tour so that my father doesn't yell at me for not doing the job right...again." Storm replied with a little sigh. Then he quickly tried to put on a fake smile. "Well then, everyone follow me!" he announced quickly, turning around and starting to move.

"Somebody must be having some daddy issues." Fury sneered, laughing at Storm. Rose was about to fuss at him for the comment, but Rainstorm had gotten to him first.

"Now come on Fury, that wasn't a very nice thing to say." Rainstorm remarked, with a strange confidence seeming to suddenly come out of nowhere. "I might be able to handle you being grumpy for a while, but I can't just let you say things like that to other dragons. Especially when they're trying to be nice to you." The face of pure shock that spread across Furys face almost made Bolt start to burst out laughing.

"What happened to the shy little dragonet we came across yesterday?" Bolt asked, a smirk spreading across his face.

"Don't listen to him." Rainstorm insisted to Storm, ignoring Bolt's comment, and giving Bolt a teasing glare. "Now Fury, I believe there is something you need to say to Storm?" She said with a smirk, glaring at Fury. Fury just stared at her, completely in shock before letting out a low growl. Then he just let out a long, exasperated sigh.

"Sorry." Fury muttered quietly, looking away from Storm.

"What was that? You will need to speak up" Rainstorm said, now beginning to tease Fury. He gave her an annoyed look, before looking back at Storm.

"Sorry." He muttered again, this time just a little bit louder.

"Still can't hear you." Rainstorm smirked, continuing to mess with him.

"I said I'm sorry alright!" he shouted before recoiling, realizing what he just did.

"There, that's much better. But there is no need for you to yell." Rainstorm smirked, completely unphased when Fury had shouted at her. "You may now continue." She said, giving Storm a little nod.

"Thank you." Storm replied, smiling at Rainstorm for how she was trying to help. Storm then looked at Fury, giving them a little smile. "And Fury, I accept your apology." Rose giggled at Rainstorm's comment as Fury turned to her with a glare.

Storm continued walking down several long hallways, explaining what each and every room was and what its purpose was. Bolt had really tried to pay attention to what Storm was saying, but he just couldn't seem to be able to get that strange dream out of his head.

What is going on with me? What was that strange amulet I saw in my dream? Why do I feel like it's trying to tell me something important? His mind spun, with question after question about what had happened last night.

"Are you ok?" Rainstorm whispered, moving over to Bolt and looking at him with a curious expression. "You look like you've seen a ghost."

"It's nothing. It's just that I had this really weird dream last night and I just can't shake off the feeling that it might have meant something." Bolt replied in a hushed voice. He then looked at Rainstorm and gave her a small smile."By the way how was last night for you? Did my brother give you any kind of trouble? I'm so sorry if he did anything that might have upset you." Bolt whispered to her, giving her an apologetic look.

"No no, he didn't do anything that really bothered me much. Sure he was a bit cranky about me being there, and only every now and then did he point out things I was doing that he didn't like.

"I actually kind of liked the fact that he did that, because it made me feel like he's not the kind of dragon who would keep all of his thoughts to himself. He doesn't pretend he likes me." She responded, giving Bolt a small smile before continuing. "It makes me think he doesn't hate being around me, unlike most dragons I have met here." She added with a long sigh. Before Bolt could say anything else Storm suddenly started speaking louder as they got to the next room. The next room seemed to be very different from the rest. A large metal door was keeping whatever was in that room locked up tight to keep anything from getting in or out.

"Now if you all look to the left you will see the royal treasury, which is filled with priceless artifacts, jewels, and other expensive materials. It is also where a very special, magical artifact, which was used to defeat Whirlwind's wicked wife, Snowstorm, is kept. Locked up until it is needed once more. It's kept in its own vault inside, just in case anything manages to get in the treasury." Storm announced. Then he stopped so that they could get a good look at the large vault door. All of a sudden Bolt began to feel a massive wave of energy begin to flow through him, almost as if something was calling to him from deep inside the vault. *What was that?* He thought to himself. *Did that come from what I think it came from?*

Yes, that was the artifact that I had used to stop Snowstorm. It's called the elemental amulet. It's the most powerful tool in thunderfang history. Whirlwind's voice replied in Bolt's head.

"The artifact has been doing very strange things in the past few days though. We can't seem to find out what's causing it to act up though, but whatever the reason, it must be really important." Storm announced, getting ready to continue to show them around.

"Hold up." Bolt said, causing Storm to pause and look back at him. "What do you mean by 'it's been acting strange'?"

"Well during the day it doesn't really do much. During the night though the artifact starts to glow brightly and it gives off a little buzz of energy, which can be felt through the ground. Why do you ask?" Storm replied, looking at Bolt with a puzzled expression.

What exactly are you planning? You have no need for a dangerous thing like that. Whirlwind's voice said in Bolt's head.

I have to check it out. What if it's important for saving the palace? What if it can show me what's going to happen so I can stop it? Bolt thought. *This could be my one chance to find out. I will just ask to see it and if anything makes me feel uneasy I will leave.*

I don't know, this doesn't sound like a very good idea. That amulet is highly unstable, I would know. His father replied. Bolt let out a long sigh, as he thought of what could happen.

Well it's not really up to you right now, is it? He thought, making up his mind about what he was going to do.

"Do you think it would be possible for us to see the artifact?" Bolt asked, looking at Storm.

"I don't see why not." Storm replied, giving Bolt a quick smile.

"My dad hardly lets me go in there though. But I guess since you're the one in charge I don't see why you shouldn't be allowed in there."

Wow. I did not think that was actually going to work as well as it did. Bolt thought, completely dumbfounded.

Neither did I... Whirlwind's voice muttered in Bolt's head.

"Please, I have no intention of taking charge and becoming king at the moment. I just want to get to know everyone for now before I do that." Bolt sighed, shaking his head.

If I do that at all. I never really saw myself as a king before. Bolt thought, a frown beginning to spread across his snout. He looked over and saw his brother glaring at him. Bolt gave him an apologetic smile before looking away. Rainstorm also saw this and slowly went up to Fury.

"Is something wrong?" Rainstorm whispered to Fury, winding her tail around his without thinking. Almost instantly Fury's gaze seemed to soften as he looked at Rainstorm and then looked down at her tail. Rainstorm followed his gaze and saw what he was looking at, turning beet red when she saw what she was doing.

"Oh! I'm so sorry! Was I making you feel uncomfortable?" Rainstorm stammered quickly, realizing what she was doing and quickly pulled her tail away, looking away in embarrassment.

"No. You weren't making me feel uncomfortable." Fury sighed, before looking back up at Bolt with a glare.

"He is the one who's making me feel uncomfortable. Everyone is treating him like he's a king, and he doesn't even want to be king! Nobody has ever treated me like that.

"If he's a prince then that means so am I. What makes everyone think that he will be the one to take the throne?" he hissed quietly, continuing to glare at Bolt with resentment. Rainstorm's nervous expression seemed to start to slowly fade when she heard what Fury had said. She then gave him an empathetic smile.

"So, what I'm hearing is that you're afraid of being left out?" she said, speaking to him in a low whisper, making sure that no one else could hear her. "Is that why you are acting like this?" she asked, looking straight into Fury's eyes.

"What!? No! I am *not* afraid of anything!" Fury hissed, stopping when he saw her flinch back. "Sorry I didn't mean to snap at you. It's just that I don't see why everything always has to be about him." He confessed, letting out a long sigh.

"I know how you feel. I mean about being left out. Not so much about the whole being king thing." Rainstorm said quickly, looking him in the eyes. "I am left out all the time here. And all because I wasn't born in the kingdom, just like you." She added in a soft voice. Fury looked at her with a confused expression as if he was trying to figure something out about her.

Why is she being so nice to me? Isn't she afraid of me? Why isn't she afraid of me like everyone else? Fury's mind spun with questions and a mix of emotions before he finally managed to speak.

"Yeah...Just like me." He repeated, his tough expression going away completely. He then looked at her with a small smile. "Look. I'm sorry about earlier. When you ran into me when we were on the way to the palace. I shouldn't have yelled at you." He said with a sigh.

"It's ok. I forgive you. It's not the first time I've been yelled at." Rainstorm replied with a smile. Then they were suddenly interrupted by the loud noise of several moving gears as Storm was finally beginning to open the metal door. Rainstorm quickly stopped what she was doing, trying to keep Storm from seeing what they were doing.

"There we go. Now let me show you where the artifact is." Storm said with a smile as the door came to a stop.

"I believe it's actually called the elemental amulet." Bolt commented without even thinking. All of a sudden Sky, Rainstorm, and Storm, looked straight at Bolt.

Oh shoot! I shouldn't have said that! Now they're probably thinking "How did he know that? He's never even been here before." Oh what do I do now, what do I do!? Bolt thought, starting to panic, trying to think of something he could say that could fix this.

"How exactly did you know that?" Storm asked, looking at Bolt with a confused expression.

"Yes Bolt. How did you know that?" Sky repeated, scowling at Bolt. "You've never been here before, so why don't you explain how you would know that. You wouldn't lie to me. Right?"

"Ooo someone's in trouble." Rose giggled, looking at Bolt with a taunting expression.

"Rose, now is not the time for this." Sky said scornfully, looking down at Rose.

Maybe I should just go while I have a chance. Bolt thought, beginning to slink away while Sky wasn't looking.

"Oh." Rose muttered quietly, looking down, feeling a bit embarrassed. When Sky looked back up she saw Bolt trying to sneak away from the crowd.

"And where exactly do you think you're going?" Sky asked, pulling him back by his tail. Bolt slowly turned around and looked at her with a nervous expression.

"N-nowhere." Bolt stuttered. "Just thought I should go stretch my wings." He added quickly, trying to think of a better excuse.

Now this is hard to watch. Honestly I think it would just be better for you to tell them the full truth now. Whirlwind muttered inside of Bolt's mind.

You're joking right? If I do that they will know that I've been lying to them! Then they would never trust me again. Bolt thought back. He then let out a little sigh. *I guess you're right. They already know something is up, and Sky is right. I shouldn't have to lie to her.*

Bolt took a deep breath and got ready to explain.

"Well. We're waiting." Sky said impatiently, tapping the end of her tail on the ground. By this point everyone else was looking at Bolt with the same confused expression.

"Fine. No more lies." Bolt sighed, looking at Sky with a look of defeat. "Do you remember when you said that the voices of the previous king's spirits could be heard?"

"Yes...?" Sky said slowly. "What about it?"

"Well you see, the night before you and I met, I had this strange dream. And a voice started talking to me in my head. At first I didn't think of it much, but then it came back the next night." Bolt confessed in a quiet voice.

"Yeah I definitely remember that. But you told us it was just a nightmare?" Rose commented, frowning at him.

"That's not all though." Bolt sighed, looking down in shame. "That night we spent under the stars the voice came yet again in my dreams and I found out it was our father." Everyone in the room let out a little gasp and stared at Bolt with bewilderment.

"Are you trying to say that Whirlwind's spirit...has been talking to you in your dreams?" Storm asked, his voice becoming very serious.

"Yes. He has been speaking with me in my dreams for the past few nights. I'm guessing it had something to do with whatever is also causing the amulet to freak out." Bolt said with a sigh, giving them an empathetic look. "Except for last night. Last night, I saw that there was nothing but darkness and the pillar that was holding the amulet.

"Then this new voice started talking to me and it seemed to come from the amulet itself. It wanted me to put it on, but as soon as I touched it a wave of pain was sent through me and I was woken up."

"Is that all?" Sky asked, softening her gaze. Everyone once again looked at Bolt, waiting for an answer.

"There is one more thing." Bolt admitted. "The very first dream that was given to me was the palace, which was burning to the ground, everyone around me going up in flames."

The group let out another gasp and started muttering to each other.

"Why didn't you tell us this sooner? Why didn't you tell me sooner?" Sky asked, giving Bolt a wounded look.

"I thought you would think I was crazy, I thought that it would ruin everything that I was trying to accomplish. I know, I should have told you sooner, but I was scared that I would lose my family." Bolt managed to choke out, trying to keep from bursting into tears.

"Yes. You should have told us sooner. But we wouldn't have hated you or thought you were crazy. We would have supported you and tried to figure out what was going on." Sky smiled, wrapping her wings around Bolt, comforting him. "I'm just glad you told us the truth, even if it took you a couple days to do."

"So is that why you wanted to see the artifact?" Storm asked, the confused expression returning to his face.

"Amulet," Bolt corrected him. "It's called an amulet. And yes, that is why I wanted to see it." Sky wiped away his tears as he reconfigured himself. "Take me to the amulet."

"As you wish." Storm said, turning over to a secondary locked door, this one looking sturdier than the first. "Here it is." He said as he began to unlock the vault door. Then Storm slowly began opening up the door. Everyone peered in and as expected, all that was in this vault was the strange pedestal from Bolt's dream. The amulet itself was on the pedestal, surrounded by a thick box of glass. Storm slowly stepped out of the way and let the group go into the vault. No sooner had Bolt gone into the doorway did the amulet start glowing with a blinding light. It began giving off a loud screeching sound, causing everyone to cover their ears.

Open the case! The strange voice from last night screeched, this time outloud, allowing everyone to hear it. Then it began rapidly spewing out strange words that none of them had ever heard before. This caused the whole group to jump in shock.

"What is it doing!" Rose shouted. "Make it stop!" she hurried out of the vault as fast as she could, her wings covering her ears, tears rolling down her cheeks.

"It's never done that before!" Storm shouted to Bolt, before leaving the vault in a panic. Everyone rushed out of the vault covering their ears.

That is, everyone except for Bolt.

"Bolt come on! What are you waiting for!?" Sky shouted, looking back at Bolt. Bolt just stared at the amulet, seeming to be in some sort of strange trance. He felt like he was being drawn closer to the amulet, reaching for the glass cover.

DONT! His father shouted in his head, but it was already too late. Bolt took the case off, reached out, grabbed the amulet, and slowly placed it around his neck.

CHAPTER

7

The vault lit up with a blinding light, so bright that everyone outside the vault had to look away. Then, the light vanished, and there was silence.

"Is it over?" Rose whimpered, tears still flowing down her cheeks. Sky wrapped her wings around Rose and pulled her in close.

"I don't know." Sky whispered quietly to Rose, before looking up into the vault. The silence was almost unbearable at this point.

"I think it's over." Storm said, peering into the vault. The vault was pitch black, every inch covered in an inky blackness.

"Do you think Bolt's alright? Should we go in and check?" Rainstorm asked, looking at Storm.

"I think that's a good idea." Sky said, creeping up to the vault door. But as soon as she had gotten to the door, Bolt came rushing out of the vault. Surprised, Sky let out a little yelp and jumped back. When she saw it was Bolt she let out a little sigh of relief. Then she slowly went up to Bolt and took a deep breath. "WHAT IS WRONG WITH YOU!" she hissed, glaring intensely at Bolt.

"W-what!?" Bolt stammered, startled and confused by Skys reaction.

"We thought you were dead!" she hissed, her glare only getting more intense as time went on. "What were you thinking!? Why didn't you leave with the rest of us!? Why did you just stand there!?"

"I don't know!" Bolt said defensively, backing away. "I wanted to run but I couldn't! It was like it was controlling me, making me put it on!"

"Wait. You put it on!" Sky said, her voice rising with both fear and anger. "Do you have any idea how dangerous that thing is!?" she looked down and saw the amulet around him. "It's what killed your father! Take it off right now!"

"Ok! Ok!" Bolt said frantically. Bolt tried to wrap his tail around the end of the amulet to try and take it off, but he couldn't seem to get under the amulet. It seemed to be burned deep into his scales. He tried to pry it off again, but the amulet still didn't budge. He tried again and again, each time with more force. The amulet still would not budge. Aggravated, Bolt tried cutting it off with the spike on his tail. The amulet refused to budge and didn't have a single scratch on it.

"Umm, I can't take it off!" Bolt said slowly, starting to panic. Sky tried to help him remove the necklace, but it didn't seem to make a difference.

"Great!" Sky said with an exasperated groan. "Now we can't get it off of you." She let out another sigh, and then she started to cry, leaning onto Bolt. "I don't want to lose you."

"You're not going to lose me." Bolt said, holding her head up, trying to comfort her. "I'm sure this isn't a bad thing." He pulled her into a hug.

"Actually, he's right." A voice commented from outside of the treasury. It was Cyclone, and he was staring right at them from outside. Everyone froze hearing his voice, then all at once they all slowly turned, facing him.

"Hey...Dad." Storm said nervously. "I thought you said you were going to be gone all day for patrol?"

"We finished early. And I'm glad we did because I wouldn't want to miss this." Cyclone chuckled before coming into the treasury.

"And what do you mean he's right?" Sky demanded. "This...Thing was what killed King Whirlwind."

"Technically, yes. It is what killed him. But, it was not the reason for his death." Cyclone said, before looking at Bolt. "The amulet takes energy whenever it's used. And in the fight with Snowstorm, Whirlwind lost almost all of his energy.

"He had to use the amulet to defeat Snowstorm which took the rest of his energy. That is what killed him." Cyclone said, moving closer to Bolt, inspecting the amulet. "It should be fine for Bolt to use, as long as he doesn't use it too much at once and sleeps in one of the static pools every night."

"Oh, so you mean he isn't going to die?" Sky asked, looking up at Cyclone with a hopeful expression. Cyclone shook his head with a smile. Sky leaned into Bolt's wings, wrapping her wings around him. "Don't you ever scare me like that again. And please just tell me before you do something so stupid." She laughed quietly, tears of joy flowing down her snout. She tightened her hug, as if she never wanted to let go of him.

"Can't...Breath." Bolt gasped.

"Oh, my bad." Sky said nervously, letting go of him. Bolt took a big breath, before looking back up at Sky with a smile.

"Wait, so now that you have the amulet, are you able to control other elements?" Storm asked, intrigued, looking at Bolt, then looking at the amulet.

I completely forgot about that. Can I now control the other elements? Bolt thought, looking down at the amulet.

Unfortunately it doesn't work like that. There are specific things one must master before they can access the amulets full potential. Whirlwind said.

"I don't know, I definitely don't feel any different." Bolt said with a shrug.

"Well why don't you try it out, let's see what happens." Storm said excitedly.

"I bet he either gets himself killed or us killed." Fury sneered quietly to Rainstorm.

"Stop being so negative, you're not helping anyone by doing that." Rainstorm whispered back to him.

"So how do I do this, do I just think of something and it happens?" Bolt asked, a look of confusion beginning to spread across his face.

Just try to imagine a glowing ember, and then imagine that ember slowly bursting into flames. The harder you picture that in your head, the stronger your control will get. But, just to warn you, the amulet also responds to emotion, and anger would work best with fire. His father said.

"Alright then, here goes nothing I guess." Bolt thought, glancing at everyone in the room. He closed his eyes and pictured a singular glowing ember. He imagined that ember glowing brighter and hotter. "I think I can feel something." He muttered. The amulet started to glow a faint red. All of a sudden, a tiny flame appeared on his scales and quickly went out. Then the amulet stopped glowing entirely and Bolt slowly opened his eyes. "Did it work?" He asked, looking at Storm.

"Kinda. It was a bit more underwhelming than I thought it would be." Storm shrugged, with a puzzled expression. Suddenly Fury burst out laughing.

"That was even better than I had imagined! You got one tiny flame for like, half a second and then poof! Nothing!" Fury sneered at Bolt, even Rainstorm and Sky couldn't help letting out a little chuckle.

"I think that was a good first attempt." Rose said, an empathetic smile on her face. "There is always next time."

"Was it really that bad?" Bolt asked, shocked and a little bit annoyed. Everyone nodded, looking at him.

"Calm down." Cyclone chuckled. "It takes time. You're not just going to be able to cause tsunamis or create mountains right off the bat. You're going to need a lot more practice with it if you want to get as good as your father." He said, patting Bolt on the back with his tail. "But, I must admit, even your father had better luck on his first attempt using this."

"Great, so what you're saying is that I basically have a magical amulet with training wheels." Bolt muttered sourly. "I don't want to spend the rest of my life training."

"Now come on, It won't take that long." Cyclone said with a smile. "But if you want to get better at it faster, you're going to have to put in a lot of effort into using it and building its power."

"That's great! That means you get to stay here with us!" Sky said with a big smile across her face. Fury let out an annoyed sigh.

"Great, now we can't leave this place." Fury said, then glanced at Rainstorm before speaking up again. "I guess it's not all bad, there are a few things here that I don't hate."

"That's the spirit!" Rose jumped up excited. "I would love to stay here. I love it here and I never want to leave. And I've already made so many new friends here!" she gave Rainstorm a hug before pulling Storm into a tight hug. Storm let out a little huff as the breath was squeezed out of him.

"Thanks, but I'm not a big fan of hugging." Storm said as Rose was still clinging to him.

"Five more minutes." Rose muttered quietly, glowing a very bright pink.

"Help...Me..." Storm choked, looking at Bolt.

"Alright, alright that's enough. I'm glad we're all happy to be staying here." Bolt said, peeling Rose off Storm. "Some of us more than others." He smirked, looking at Rose.

Rose let out a little nervous chuckle as her face began to turn red.

They left the treasury and Storm locked the door behind them.

"Well now that's over with, there is only one other place I have to show you." Storm said, looking at the group.

"Actually I think I will show you this one." Cyclone said. "I'm pretty sure Storm has gotten into enough trouble for today." Storm gave a nervous laugh before moving back. Cyclone went down a long hallway which led to a flight of stairs that seemed to go deep underground. The others followed him stopping at the stairwell.

"This is creepy." Rose shuttered looking down the flight of stairs. "If only there was a dragon here who could help me be brave." She said out loud, glancing at Storm.

"Sure, I would love to." Bolt smirked, going beside Rose. Rose scowled at him, before looking away in embarrassment.

They followed Cyclone down the flight of stairs which seemed to never end. The farther they went the colder it got. Bolt shuddered as he saw that ice was starting to form on the walls.

"It's really cold down here." Rainstorm shivered. She stopped when she felt Furys wing go across her. She looked at him and barely saw Fury smile before he quickly turned his head. Bolt moved closer to Fury and gave him a teasing smile.

"You're being awfully nice today. Is there any reason for this strange behavior?" Bolt said, looking at his brother.

"It's none of your business." Fury hissed glaring at his brother. "I'm just in a good mood, ok?"

"Mhm, and did your good mood start when you ran into a certain someone?" Bolt teased. Fury hissed at him and looked away.

"I've never been down here before. What could possibly be so important that they would have to hide it all the way down here?" Sky shivered from both fear and the cold air surrounding them. She leaned onto Bolt, wrapping her tail around his as they reached the bottom of the stairs. Cyclone stopped and looked back at the group.

"This is where we keep the biggest threat to our kingdom, Snowstorm. We keep it freezing down here so that the ice keeping her trapped doesn't melt." Cyclone said walking over to a large door made out of a strange kind of metal Bolt had never seen before.

Cyclone grabbed his spear, placing the spike into an indentation on the door. Streaks of electricity flowed out of the spear into the frame of the door. The loud sound of gears could be heard as the door slowly cracked open. He removed the spear and opened the door the rest of the way.

"Woah." Everyone said entering the room. The room was covered in a thick sheet of ice, a massive block of ice in the middle. Inside of the ice was the dragon Bolt had seen in his dream. It was Snowstorm, frozen in ice, with a look of pure hatred in her eyes.

CHAPTER

8

"Who is that?" Rose asked with a look of confusion and fear on her face as she stared at the frozen dragon. Storm was about to speak up, but Bolt beat him to it.

"That's Snowstorm, our mother. She is the reason our father is dead." Bolt said with a low hiss, glaring at the frozen dragon. *She is the reason we had to live in hiding in that awful cave. She is the reason for all the bad things that have happened to us.* Bolt thought, furious. His mind started replaying their life in the cave. Always afraid of being found.

Bolt was so wrapped up in thought, he didn't even notice that the amulet was slowly starting to glow a faint red. It continued to glow, gradually getting brighter. Eventually Cyclone glanced over and saw what was happening. He quickly hurried over to Bolt, staring directly at him.

"Bolt, whatever you are thinking about, you need to stop thinking about it right now. I need you to take deep breaths and try to calm down and relax." Cyclone warned, trying to use a comforting tone to try and calm down Bolt. All this did was make Bolt grow more agitated, which caused the amulet to begin to glow even brighter. All of a sudden the air around them started getting warmer and warmer, the ice on the walls started to fog up and begin to melt.

Who does he think he is, telling me what to do? I'm the king for crying out loud! I don't have to listen to anyone! They should be the ones listening to me! Bolt's mind spun with all these thoughts and feelings. Bolt didn't know why, but for some reason it felt like all this anger started bubbling inside of him, seeming to come from nowhere.

He began to grow angry at his mother for ruining his life, angry at his brother, who did nothing but get in his way and complain. But most importantly, angry at himself, for not doing something about this sooner, for keeping them locked up in a cave when they could have gone anywhere they wanted to.

Bolt, you need to clear your mind, these are not your true feelings. The amulet seems to be twisting your sense of emotion. Whirlwind said in a calm tone.

Bolt ignored his father, too focused on the anger that was swelling up inside of him. The amulet kept glowing brighter and brighter as the temperature around him continued to rise. The block of ice that was containing Snowstorm started to melt and crack.

"Bolt! I need you to calm down! The amulet is responding to your anger and feeding off of it to gain power! You have to calm down or you could set this entire room ablaze!" Cyclone shouted, panicking, trying to think of what to do. Then all of a sudden, Bolt felt Sky wrapping her tail around his tail. Sky turned around and faced him, staring directly into his eyes.

"Please, Bolt, we need you to calm down. I know you're angry, but being angry will not solve anything.

"If you do not calm down you will release the very thing that ruined your life in the first place. Please Bolt, you have to calm down, for me." Sky whispered in a soft, calming voice, not looking away from Bolt's eyes.

Sky is right...What am I doing? I am better than this, I can't let my emotions get the better of me. I am in control...I am in control...I...am in...control. Bolt thought, the onslaught of memories of their life in the cave beginning to slow. *I am focusing on the bad things that have happened. But now I need to look at the good things. I grew up with a family who loved me. I got to watch them grow, becoming the dragons they are today.*

Flashbacks of Rose and Fury appeared in his head as he closed his eyes.

"Catch me if you can!" Rose shouted playfully as she flew around their cave. Bolt was following her with a big smile on his face as he began to gain on her.

"I'm gonna getcha!" Bolt said, smiling. He ran into Rose and they both fell to the ground laughing. "I told you I would get you." He laughed getting back up again.

"Now it's my turn to chase you!" Rose said, getting up again as Bolt started flying around their cave. She looked at Fury who was sitting in the corner.

"Come on Fury, join us, you're always saying how much faster than us you are." She smiled going up to Fury.

"Ok! But you'll never be able to catch up to me!" Fury said with a grin.

The flashback faded as Bolt began to slowly calm down, trying to fight against the feelings that the amulet was forcing him to have. The glow had started to slowly dim and the area around Bolt was gradually starting to cool back down.

"Yes! Whatever you're doing I want you to keep on doing it!" Sky shouted with joy as she smiled at Bolt, wrapping her wings around him. The ice block containing Snowstorm slowly began to stop melting and cracking. Bolt's eyes were still shut tight, as he tried to regain himself.

I met my father, and found out who I really was. Bolt thought, as his very first vision began to replay in his head. The image of his father appeared in his head.

You're doing great, son. Just slow your breathing and continue to think of all the good things. Whirlwind said in Bolt's head. Then an image of Sky appeared in his head as the flow of emotions suddenly stopped, seeming to have faded entirely.

And...I met Sky. The dragonet who makes me feel whole. The one that makes me feel like I could do nothing wrong. Bolt thought, as the day they had first met started to replay in his head. *Ever since that day, she has never left my side. She forgave me for all the lies I've told her. And now she is right in front of me, waiting for me to do the right thing.*

All of a sudden he felt her scales press against his as she pulled him into a tight hug. Then she did something that Bolt would never have expected. She laid her head down on his shoulders and Bolt could hear her breathing, time seeming to come to a complete stop, and all he could hear was her voice.

"You have to calm down." Sky whispered in a soothing voice. "I can't lose you like this. You mean the world to me. You *are* my world." She said, her voice started to shake. Bolt had a feeling that he knew exactly where this was going. All the bad feelings began disappearing rapidly as the glow from the amulet faded to a dim little shimmer. "What I'm trying to say is...I-I love you." She managed to say, in a quiet, hushed voice. Bolt's heart started beating faster than it ever had before and all of a sudden it felt like the only ones here were him, and Sky. Bolt's mind started filling with powerful emotions and he began to think of the past couple of days with Sky.

This is what that strange feeling must have been. This is why I feel so calm around her. This is my chance." Bolt thought. He took a deep breath as he put his wings around Sky.

"I love you too." He whispered, opening his eyes, a big smile on his face. The amulet stopped glowing entirely and the heat that was emanating from Bolt completely vanished.

The room fell silent as Sky let go of Bolt and the two of them looked at each other and then back at the group. Then, all at once, everyone started moving in closer to them, wrapping their wings around Bolt and Sky. Everyone that is, except for Fury. Bolt glanced at his brother and saw the nervous expression on his face.

He is worried that he won't be welcome here. Bolt realized, giving his brother an empathetic look. "Oh get over here, you know you want to." He said with a smile gesturing for his brother to come and join them. Fury gave him an expression of utter confusion, staring at Bolt like he had just grown a second head.

"Thank you, for the offer I mean, but I am not much of a hugger." Fury said, his tensed expression easing slightly.

"Oh get over here you big grumpy serpent." Rainstorm laughed, practically pulling Fury into the hug with her tail. Fury let out a little umph as he was pulled into the group. Then he let out a little sigh and wrapped his tail around Rainstorms.

"Thank you." he whispered quietly to Rainstorm, giving her a warm smile.

"I knew that part of you was in there somewhere." She said, smiling back at him. After a while everyone began to pull themselves together. Then they looked at the ice on the walls, which had almost melted completely.

"I hope we weren't too late." Storm sighed, looking back at Bolt. "How do you feel?" he asked, looking for any possible injuries. Everyone began to look at Bolt, waiting for him to answer.

"I feel fine. Kind of tired and maybe a little bit embarrassed, but overall I feel fine." Bolt answered, looking right at Sky with a big smile.

"No anger? Nothing else like that?" Storm asked, studying Bolt's face.

"No nothing like that." Bolt said, shaking his head.

"I think it would probably be for the best if we left this area." Cyclone said, heading back up the stairs. Everyone nodded and one by one everyone started going up the stairs. Everyone except for Bolt and Sky, who just stayed there, looking around nervously.

"Well then, this is a bit awkward, is this awkward for you?" Sky asked nervously, giving Bolt a quick glance. Bolt just stared back at her with a smile.

"Did you really mean what you said back there?" Bolt asked, giving her a hopeful smile. "Or did you just say it because you knew it would calm me down?"

"Well, I, um." Sky said, stuttering, looking away trying to hide her blush. She then took a deep breath and turned back to face Bolt. "Yes, I meant every word of it. What about you?"

"I meant it. At least I am pretty sure I meant it. I can't tell if it was my actual feelings, or if it was the amulet giving me those feelings. I really don't like this thing. How am I supposed to know what I am truly feeling?" Bolt muttered, looking at the amulet that had attached itself to him. The amulet wasn't giving off any sort of glow now, and if he didn't know better, he would have thought it was just an ordinary piece of jewelry.

"Well either way, I am still glad you told me. The amulet doesn't give you emotions you don't already have, it just boosts the ones you are currently feeling." Sky said, smiling at him, giving him another big hug.

"Well, come on you two, hurry it up, we don't have all day!" Fury shouted from the top of the stairs.

"Alright, alright, we're on our way, don't get your tail tied in a knot." Bolt shouted back up at his brother. Bolt looked back and took one final glance at the frozen dragon. *Goodbye mother.* He thought, before going up the stairs with Sky, their tails still intertwined. By the time the two had gotten back up the stairs, Rose was already moving around, excited, looking at the two of them with a big smile on her face.

"Well would you look at that. I was right." Rose smirked, looking at the two dragonets. "I knew that you had a thing for her!" she laughed, before looking at Bolt with a teasing expression. Sky gave her a little smile before turning away as she began to blush.

"Fine, you were right about this *one* thing." Bolt smirked, messing with his sister.

"One thing!?" Rose said, giving Bolt a silly glare before bursting into another fit of laughter.

I told you that you two would be great for each other. Whirlwind said in a taunting tone. *One point for me, zero for you.*

"Alright, alright, go ahead and get it out of your system." Bolt said with a smirk, looking at Rose and then back at Sky. *You too.* He thought, responding to his father.

"Well then, I do believe that this concludes our tour." Cyclone said. "I think I should probably start getting back to my station. I just have one rule that I want you to follow while I'm gone." He said, looking at Bolt "I don't want any of you to go back into that room, more importantly I don't want Bolt to go back into that room, at least not until he's learned how to control the amulet, instead of letting it control him, and remember-"

"Practice, practice, practice. I know, I know, I will." Bolt sighed, looking down at the amulet again.

"Good, I will be back by tomorrow morning to help you with your training." Cyclone said, looking directly at Bolt before flying away.

"Well that was...something." Storm muttered slowly, looking back at Bolt. "I've heard some stories about the amulet. Although none of them mentioned being able to do anything remotely similar to what you just did."

"What do you mean?" Bolt asked, giving Storm a puzzled look. "The amulet allows me to control the elements, isn't that what I just did?"

"Yeah you can control the other elements, but others have never been able to change their bodies like that, or change the environment around them like you did." Storm said, inspecting the amulet around Bolt's neck. "How did you get it to do that?"

"I don't know, I just got angry at my mother and then all of sudden that anger just kept growing and growing for no reason. Then I started having all these flashbacks and images of what it was like living in our cave, and it was showing me every bad thing that had happened to us." Bolt said, looking at his brother and sister before looking back at Storm.

"But then you just...stopped. How did you do that?" Storm asked, getting a closer inspection of the amulet. He poked at the different gemstones before moving back and looking at Bolt with a confused expression.

"Well I just started to think of all the good things that had happened to us while we lived in that cave. It seemed to slow the bad thoughts down. And then…I thought of Sky, and how I had met her. That caused all the bad thoughts to go away almost instantly." Bolt responded, looking back at Sky with a smile.

Sky returned the smile and leaned against him. Storm started pacing back and forth, thinking about what Bolt had said before stopping, coming to a conclusion.

"So we do know that the amulet responds to emotions to gain power, right? Well, what if it doesn't just respond to the current emotion of the user, but also the strongest emotion that it can find!

"So that would mean that when Sky started speaking with you the amulet must have transferred to the emotion that you were feeling the most!" Storm said, a big smile across his face. "This could change everything we knew about the amulet and its powers!"

"So the amulet chose to draw power from all Bolt's sappy feelings about Sky instead of all the rage." Rose muttered slowly. "See I knew you liked her!" she said, beginning to laugh before looking at Bolt again.

"Ok ok! We all know that I like Sky, you don't have to keep pointing that out!" Bolt shouted, annoyed and embarrassed. "Anyways it's not like I'm the only one who likes another dragonet here." He smirked, looking at his sister before looking at Storm. This quickly got Rose to stop laughing as she started to blush, giving Bolt a quick glare. Storm just looked around, confused.

"I don't get it?" He asked, looking at Bolt and then at Rose.

"It's nothing!" Rose said quickly, before looking at Bolt. "Say, you must be so tired from using the amulet. Why don't you go and get some sleep." She announced, glaring at him.

Bolt shook his head with a little chuckle before giving Rose an amused smile.

"I am tired, yes, but it's only the afternoon." Bolt said, giving Rose a little smirk.

"Oh, I know! We can eat at my place. My parents would love to meet you. They would be so proud of me for finding the royal family's lost dragonets!" Sky declared excitedly, pulling Bolt, Rose, and Fury close. Fury quickly pulled himself out of the little group hug, and faced Sky with a mix of a scowl and a smile.

"As much as we would love to do that, I think I will stay with Rainstorm for a while. Maybe I can get everyone else to start respecting her and treating her like everyone else." He replied with a scowl, slowly moving closer to Rainstorm, who simply just smiled at him.

"I'm sure you can do that later, but just not in any violent kind of way." Rainstorm smiled, looking at Fury with soft eyes. "But I really think you should go, it would be the kind thing to do." Fury let out a little annoyed groan before turning to face Sky.

"Fine, I guess I can come along for this one thing since it is the least I could do." Fury muttered sourly, glaring at Bolt.

"That's great!" Sky shouted, giving Fury a quick hug and getting ready to fly.

"Hold up." Bolt insisted, coming up beside her. "Are you absolutely sure that this is a good idea?" He asked, looking at her with a worried expression. He flinched as Sky flicked his snout with the end of her tail and smirked at him.

"What did I say about you worrying about things too much." She said, teasing him. "It will be fine. Trust me, we have a spare room with a few static pools in case you decide to stay the night."

"Wait, hold up, I never said anything about staying the night!" Fury interjected quickly, looking over to where Rainstorm was staying.

"Too late, you already said you would come." Sky smirked. Bolt slowly moved over to his brother.

"Oh come on, it won't be that bad. Don't tell me you're scared of a little sleepover?" Bolt teased, poking at his brother.

"I am *not* scared." Fury hissed, pushing Bolt away.

"Great! Then follow me!" Sky said, taking off into the sky. As they flew off, a guard poked his head from around a corner.

"I should probably make sure the ice down there is still secure." The guard muttered to himself. He went down into the chamber and inspected the cracks in the ice. He looked at the frozen block that Snowstorm was trapped in. *It should be fine. I don't see any large cracks or chunks missing.* The guard thought, turning around to go back up the stairs. He stopped as he heard a little creak coming from behind him. He turned around to see what it was, but didn't see anything out of the ordinary.

He shrugged and turned around, heading towards the stairs. Right as he got to the stairs he let out a little yelp as something plunged through his back. He looked down and saw a long spike of ice sticking out of his chest. The guard dropped to the ground as the spike was pulled out of his back. The last thing he saw was Snowstorm's eyes staring right at him from inside the block of ice.

CHAPTER

9

They continued flying until they reached the outskirts of the town. The buildings there were clustered together with very little room around them. They looked old and worn down, ready to collapse at any moment.

"Woah, what happened down here?" Rose asked, flying up beside Sky, giving her a puzzled look.

"Nothing happened, this is just where the scouts live. I know it's not the best place to live, but at least we have a roof over our heads." Sky replied, a hint of sorrow could be heard in her voice. Bolt looked at Sky with an empathetic look.

"Why would they just keep dragons in a place like this? Whose awful idea was this? I don't see why you would need to place dragons into categories like this." Bolt said with a frown, looking at the clustered buildings. "Things are going to change, I will find a way to get rid of this whole category thing." Sky looked back at him with a smile.

"I know you will." She said, smiling at him, touching his wing with hers.

"I personally don't see what's wrong with this place." Fury commented, looking at the broken down buildings.

"Well not all of us like hiding in the shadows." Rose said, annoyed, glaring at Fury. "I don't see how it's fair that you have to live in this place when others get to live with wealth and you know, a better house." Rose frowned. "But I bet this place could look beautiful if you just add a bit of color and fix up some other things."

"Oh I'm sure everyone would love being blinded by a wave of bright pink when they go home." Sky chuckled, giving Rose a little smile. The group came to a halt as Sky stopped at an old blueish gray building covered in cobwebs that spread all over every nook and cranny of the building.

"Well this is it." Sky said, forcing a smile. "Welcome to my home." Sky flew down to the building and knocked on the door. "Mom! Dad! I'm home!" she shouted.

"Sky!?" a faint voice could be heard from inside the building. Bolt could hear shuffling around and what sounded like some kind of pottery breaking. The voice muttered something before things went silent again. Then after a while, the door opened and two dragons were at the doorway. "Sky! I can't believe it's you!" the first one shouted, wrapping their wings around Sky and pulling her close.

"When you didn't come back from patrol we thought something had happened to you!" the other dragon said, wrapping their wings around Sky as well. Sky pulled back out of their hug with a big smile.

"Actually something did happen to me." Sky muttered nervously, looking up at her parents.

"What! What happened? Are you alright?" one of them asked frantically, stretching out Sky's wings looking for any sort of injuries. Sky pulled back with a laugh.

"Mom! I'm fine! Sure I was attacked by a dune scorpion and I could have died, but luckily, someone was there to save me." She replied, looking back at Bolt with a smile. Sky's parents looked up and saw who Sky was looking at and then saw the group that was with her.

"Why don't you and your friends come inside, we can introduce each other there." Sky's mother insisted, pulling the group inside. Fury hissed, glaring at Sky's mother when she dragged him inside.

"I am perfectly capable of entering a building by myself." Fury snarled. Sky gave him a quick glare and Fury sighed. "I mean, thank you for letting us into your home." He said sourly.

"Much better." Sky smiled at Fury. "Don't mind him, he is always like that." Sky's parents brought the group into a room with a large circular table in the middle of it.

"Wow this place is so much better than our cave!" Rose observed, her voice filled with excitement. "Not as good as the palace, but definitely better than our old cave."

"Thank you?" Sky's mother said, giving Sky a confused look.

"It means she likes it." Sky whispered to her mother.

"Ok then, now that we are inside let us go ahead and introduce ourselves." Sky's father said as the group began to get comfortable. "My name is Typhoon and that is my wife, Aurora." Aurora nodded at the group before putting her wing around Sky.

"And you must obviously know our little angel, Sky." Aurora added, smiling down at Sky. Sky moved out from under Aurora's wing and blushed.

"Mom! You're embarrassing me in front of my friends!" Sky muttered sheepishly, her face turning red with embarrassment.

"Oh and that would just be the end of the world wouldn't it." Aurora replied sarcastically, a smile on her face.

"Now. Who might you three be?" Typhoon asked, looking at Bolt, Rose, and Fury. Before any of them could speak, Sky spoke up, stopping them.

"That's Rose." She said, pointing at Rose, who was currently going all around the room, excited about exploring a new place. "As you can see, she is very energetic." Sky said, Sky's parents looked at Rose and then back at Sky with an amused look.

"She has about the same energy as you did when you were younger." Aurora said, smiling at Sky. Sky looked away, starting to blush again, before she continued to introduce everyone.

"That's Fury. You already got a glimpse at what he's like. He isn't grumpy all the time, he's quite normal when he's around a certain dragonet." Sky smirked, pointing at Fury with her tail. "He might act tough but he's completely harmless." She teased.

"Completely harmless! I am *not* completely harmless!" Fury hissed, glaring at Sky. Sky ignored him and turned to face Bolt.

"And that's Bolt. He's the one that saved me from the dune scorpion." Sky said with a big smile, moving over to Bolt. Sky's parents pulled Bolt into a hug.

"Thank you for keeping our little angel safe." Aurora said, smiling at Bolt. Then both Aurora and Typhoon looked down at Bolt's tail and gasped.

"Oh yeah, I forgot to tell you, I found the last remnants of the royal family!" Sky said with excitement, looking at her parents with a big smile. Sky's parents let Bolt out of the hug and looked at him with amazement.

"You're from the royal family! How!? Everyone thought the royal family had died out!" Typhoon said, staring at the spike on Bolt's tail.

Then their eyes looked up at the amulet around Bolt's neck, their eyes widened with fear as they saw it.

"What is that *thing* doing here!?" Aurora shouted. "Get it away from here before it kills us all!" Bolt backed away slowly, shocked from their reaction.

"Wait! Everyone just calm down! It's ok, Bolt knows how to control it." Sky said quickly, rushing over to Bolt. "Mostly, at least."

"I think control is a bit of a stretch." Bolt interjected nervously, glancing at the scared expressions on Aurora's and Typhoon's face. Then Fury let out a little laugh.

"A bit of a stretch? You almost cooked us all alive!" Fury sneered. Sky turned around and glared at him.

"Not. Helping." Sky hissed at Fury. Fury stopped laughing and rolled his eyes. "But yes, he did almost do that, but he was able to stop it from happening. And Cyclone has promised to help train Bolt to teach him to get better at controlling the amulet." Sky's parents started to calm back down and gave Bolt an apologetic look.

"We're so sorry about that. It's just that what you're wearing has done more bad than good in our kingdom." Typhoon apologized, looking at Bolt.

"So...mom, I was wondering if they could stay the night. They could use our spare room." Sky asked slowly, looking up at her mother. Aurora let out a little laugh.

"Sky that is a nice offer, but I'm sure they wouldn't want to sleep in our broken down home." Aurora replied, shaking her head.

"We don't mind at all. We would love to stay the night!" Rose said excitedly.

"Since when do you speak for all of us?" Fury hissed, glaring at his sister. Bolt pricked him with his tail and gave him a stern look.

"What he meant to say, is that we would love to stay the night, and we couldn't be happier about it." Bolt said, looking back at Aurora. Aurora gave them a look of surprise before shrugging her shoulders.

"Ok I guess that settles it. There are a few static pools in the room in the back. Feel free to use those." Typhoon said, looking at Aurora before looking back at the group.

"I'll go make something for us to eat." Aurora announced, going into another room. "How does everyone feel about fish?" she asked, poking her head back around the corner.

"That would be great." Bolt replied. He saw Rose start moving around uncomfortably and looked at her.

"Yeah, I don't mind fish." Rose muttered quietly.

She must really be trying to impress them if she is willing to go through with doing this. Bolt thought, feeling bad for his sister. Sky also saw the look on Rose's face.

"You really want to do this? I can ask if they have any fruit." Sky whispered to Rose, giving her a little smile. Rose shook her head.

"No, I'll be fine." Rose said quietly, looking away.

"And what about you?" Aurora asked, looking at Fury. Fury just let out a little snort and went into the spare room.

"That means yes." Bolt interjected, giving Aurora an apologetic look.

"Great! I'll get a few fish ready for everyone." Aurora said, going back into the kitchen. Bolt looked at Sky and started heading into the spare room to talk with his brother. Sky held him back with her tail, looking at him.

"You stay out here, I'll talk to Fury this time." Sky insisted, smiling at him. Bolt opened his mouth about to say something, but then stopped and just nodded his head. He watched as Sky went into the spare room and found Fury, laying in the farthest pool in the corner of the room. She went up to Fury and looked at him. Fury saw her approaching and let out a little hiss.

"What do you want?" he hissed, glaring at Sky.

"I just want to talk." Sky said calmly. "I know you're not the best with first impressions, or second, just impressions in general.

"But I would really like it if you would just try to be nice around my parents. And that's what Rainstorm would want you to do too." Fury let out a long sigh before getting out of the shallow pool. "If you can manage this one thing I'm sure Rainstorm would be so proud of you." Sky smiled at him.

"Are you sure?" Fury asked quietly, looking at Sky with a hopeful expression. Sky nodded and Fury let out another long sigh. "I can try, but I'm not going to make any promises."

"Thank you." Sky said, smiling at him before leaving the room.

Aurora had managed to find a few large fish and was already getting ready to prepare them. Bolt went into the kitchen to see Aurora muttering to herself.

"Is everything alright?" Bolt asked, coming up to Aurora. Aurora looked up with an annoyed expression and shook her head.

"Nothing around here works anymore, I hope everyone is ok with raw fish." She sighed. Bolt gave her a confused look.

Have they been cooking their food? I always thought we just ate what we caught, cooked or not. Then again we didn't have a way to cook anything, so we didn't have much of a choice. Bolt thought, staring at the fish. *Wait, maybe I can help with this.*

"Hey can I try something? Maybe it might help." Bolt said, giving Aurora a small smile. "As a thank you for letting us stay the night."

"Sure. I don't know how you would be able to help though." Aurora muttered, shaking her head. She stepped back and let Bolt try to help.

What are you doing? Whirlwind asked. *Do you not remember what happened last time? You could barely create a spark.*

Oh yeah, very helpful. Bolt thought sarcastically. *It's the least I can do. And anyways it would be good practice.* Bolt closed his eyes and concentrated. He thought of a glowing ember, slowly glowing brighter. The amulet started to glow a faint red, but as expected nothing happened.

Ugh why wont this thing work!? Wait, maybe if I try something else. Bolt thought. He stopped thinking about the ember and pictured the fish in front of him. He imagined that the air around the fish began to heat up. The amulet started to glow even brighter. Bolt imagined all that heat being focused into one area.

Then he imagined a small fire appearing in front of the fish. He heard Aurora let out a little gasp and he slowly opened his eyes. To his amazement, he saw a small fire dancing above the fish. Sky came into the kitchen and let out a loud surprised gasp, seeing what Bolt was doing.

"Bolt! What are you doing!" Sky shouted, giving Bolt a look of both fear and frustration. She went over there to try to stop him but Bolt shook his head.

"I got this, you don't need to worry." Bolt insisted, giving Sky a big smile. The fire that was now above the fish, slowly cooking it, waved at her. Sky looked at it with a confused expression and then looked at Bolt.

"You did that? You're controlling the fire?" Sky asked, amused. Then Rose came into the kitchen and her eyes widened with awe.

"Wow! You're controlling fire! I knew you had it in you!" Rose said, moving around excitedly, trying to get a closer look. Bolt smiled as the fire hovered above the fish as he finished cooking the fish.

"That was the coolest thing I've ever seen!" Rose said excitedly, looking at Bolt. "Now...how do you turn it off?" she asked with a curious expression. Bolt was about to ask his father.

Don't look at me. I've never seen anyone control it the way you are. Whirlwind said.

"Um...I don't...know." Bolt muttered slowly. He tried to picture the flame disappearing, but when he opened his eyes the flame was still there.

Hmm, what do I do now? Bolt thought, beginning to panic. Bolt then pictured the heat around the flame dispersing, picturing the flame getting smaller and smaller. He then imagined the fire being put out, the only thing left being a small wisp of smoke. When Bolt opened his eyes again he saw that the flame was gone. *I can't believe I just did that.* Bolt thought with amazement.

"Well then, I guess that means dinner is ready." Aurora said with a smile before looking at Bolt. "Thank you." She said with an appreciative smile. She brought the fish to the table and called out for everyone. The room smelled of cooked fish, making Bolt's mouth water. Fury came out of the spare room and Bolt swore he saw his brother smile as the smell of the food washed over him.

Fury sat down in front of the table, reaching out to grab one of the fish before he saw the look on Sky's eyes. He let out a sigh before moving up close, in between his brother and sister. Fury waited for Typhoon to give everyone a fish, before starting to eat.

Wow, Fury has definitely changed since we came here. If we were back at our cave he would have just snatched one of the fish and went back to his little corner. Whatever Rainstorm is doing, she must be doing it right. Bolt thought, giving his brother a quick smile. Then he remembered Rose and looked back at her, trying to figure out what she might have been thinking. She was just staring at the fish, then she slowly leaned down and took a bite. She shivered as she swallowed before looking back up at Aurora.

"It's great." Rose managed to say, trying to force a smile. Aurora and Typhoon looked at her with puzzled expressions.

"Is everything alright with her?" Aurora whispered to Sky.

"She doesn't like to eat meat. She thinks it's wrong to kill another living creature." Sky responded, looking at her mother.

"Oh I had no idea!" Aurora said, giving Rose a sympathetic look. "Why didn't you tell us? We had a garden in the back if you wanted something from there."

"I just didn't want to hurt your feelings. And I didn't want you to think I was weird." Rose muttered quietly, pushing away the fish.

"You poor thing, we wouldn't have thought you were weird. We used to know many dragons like you that didn't like to eat meat." Aurora said, smiling at Rose. "Typhoon, do you mind getting some mangoes from the back for her?" she asked, looking at Typhoon.

"Not at all." Typhoon said, smiling at Rose as he went into the back. He came back a few minutes later with a few small mangoes. He brought them to the table giving one to Rose. "There you go, I'm sorry we didn't ask about this earlier." Typhoon said with a smile. Rose grabbed the mango and smiled back at Typhoon and Aurora.

"Thank you." Rose said with a big smile as she bit into the mango. When they had finished eating Sky went into the back to help her parents clean up. Then Sky came back over to the three of them.

"My parents say it's time to head to bed. And you could use a lot of rest after what you've done today." Sky said, looking at Bolt. "You must be really tired from using the amulet."

"I am. Thank you for bringing us to your house. Your parents are good dragons and they should be proud of you." Bolt smiled, heading back to the spare room. He went over to one of the pools and felt Sky's wing go around him. He turned around and saw her giving him a warm smile.

"I'm glad you came." Sky smiled, wrapping her tail around his.

"I am too." Bolt said, smiling back at her. He got into the shallow pool, laying his head down. "Goodnight Sky." He whispered, smiling at her.

"Goodnight Bolt." Sky smiled, wrapping her tail around his. Then she left the room and headed over to her own room. After a while Bolt fell into a calming sleep, exhausted from the day.

CHAPTER

10

Bolt woke up with a yawn as he slowly opened his eyes. The drowsiness from yesterday was completely gone. He looked down at the pool in amazement before getting out.

Wow this thing really does work. Bolt thought, amazed. *But how does it work?* He thought bewildered. Bolt looked around the pool trying to figure out what allowed it to contain and restore their energy. He looked around and saw that Rose and Fury were still asleep. *I probably shouldn't wake them up.* He smiled looking at them. He poked his head out of the room and looked around. He went out of the room and saw that Sky was in the kitchen. She was humming to herself as she was preparing something. Bolt snuck up into the kitchen and began silently creeping up behind Sky. As soon as he got close, Sky wacked him in the snout with her tail, turning around with a silly little smirk.

"You're going to have to try harder than that if you want to scare me." Sky said, amused. Bolt rubbed his snout and went beside her, looking at what she was making.

"I didn't know you could cook." Bolt said, looking at Sky.

"I had to learn how to cook, since I would be the one going out to hunt and find other fruits and vegetables." Sky replied with a sigh, looking at Bolt. "It's hard trying to get food for your family when you live in this part of the town. It's even harder when we're supposed to stay hidden when we go outside of the mountain." Sky stopped, looking at Bolt. "Do you think you could-" She started

"Oh! Yeah. I don't mind." Bolt interjected, giving her a small smile. He began to concentrate, the amulet starting to glow red. A small fire appeared above the food, cooking it slowly.

"So, how was last night? Did you have any good dreams?" Bolt said, trying to break the ongoing silence.

"I don't really remember my dreams." Sky muttered, before looking at Bolt. "What about you? Did you have any interesting dreams you should tell me about?" she asked with a hopeful smile.

"No, I didn't have any strange dreams last night. I, for once in the past few days, had a relaxing night." Bolt said, shaking his head. Soon the house began to fill with the scent of the food. Sky's parents soon came into the kitchen, followed closely by Rose and Fury.

"Breakfast is ready!" Sky said with a smile, the flame quickly disappearing. They sat around the table getting ready to eat. Then right as they started eating, they stopped, looking towards the door, hearing the sound of many wings flapping, coming closer.

"I wonder who that could be?" Typhoon said, looking at Sky.

"I'll go check." Bolt said, heading to the door. When he opened the door he saw Cyclone waiting patiently out there, several guards accompanying him.

"Rainstorm told me you would be here." Cyclone said to Bolt, with a serious expression on his face.

"Cyclone, what are you doing here?" Bolt asked as Sky came up beside him.

"There was a bit of trouble at our kingdom's border. King Scorpius sent out a few messengers and they said he wants to have the chance to speak with you in the next couple of days. We need to get you ready." Cyclone announced, looking at Bolt. Bolt looked at him with a confused stare.

"It takes a few days just to get prepared to meet somebody?" Bolt asked, confused.

"King Scorpius is one of the most dangerous rulers out there." Cyclone said. "We need to get you more used to your new amulet just in case he decides to attack." Aurora came over looking at Cyclone, then she looked at Bolt and Sky.

"I think it's time for you to go. Feel free to come back anytime you want." She said, smiling at them. Bolt called for his brother and sister. They came up and saw Cyclone.

"Oh, hi Cyclone." Rose said cheerfully. "What are you doing here? Is Storm with you?" she asked, looking around, hoping to see Storm amongst the other guards.

"We need you to come back to the palace. Just for a while until things get sorted out." Cyclone said with a smile.

"Oh, ok!" Rose responded excitedly, looking up at Cyclone with a big smile. The four of them lifted off into the sky, followed by guards, as they flew back to the palace. Bolt flew up beside Sky, looking at her.

"Who exactly is King Scorpius?" Bolt asked her, looking at her with a puzzled expression.

"King Scorpius is the leader of the dune scorpions. He is the one that sent the dune scorpion that attacked me to the jungle. He has been trying to take over our kingdom and the jungle for years now." Sky responded with a sigh. "He is why we have to stay hidden." Bolt let out a little hiss hearing that.

"He thinks he can just take my home! Does he think he can just get away with attacking my friends! He should be the one worried about meeting me, not the other way around." Bolt snarled. The amulet started glowing red again and Bolt had to try to calm himself down. Cyclone looked back and saw Bolt and waited for him.

"Calm down. We don't want a repeat of yesterday." Cyclone said, giving Bolt a nervous glance.

"I know, I know. I'm trying to calm down." Bolt muttered quietly as the amulet stopped glowing. When they got to the palace, Cyclone had the other guards disperse. As they got back on the ground he turned around facing Bolt.

"Now have you been practicing like I suggested?" Cyclone asked, staring at Bolt with a serious expression. Bolt nodded his head.

"Yeah! Last night he created a little fire and made it wave at us and use it to help Sky." Rose said, jumping up and down with excitement. Cyclone gave Bolt a skeptical look.

"Is this true?" Cyclone asked Bolt, with a look of doubt.

"Yes, it is true, I did do that. Why do you ask? Was I not supposed to do that?" Bolt asked, starting to get nervous. Sky saw the nervous expression on Bolt's face and stepped in.

"So, was there anything wrong with him helping me and my family out?" Sky asked, glaring at Cyclone.

"No, there is nothing wrong with that. But if this is true, you wouldn't mind showing me, would you?" Cyclone insisted, looking back at Bolt.

"I can try." Bolt stammered.

"Then follow me to the room you will be training at." Cyclone said, going down one of the coradoors. They followed him into a large open area that reminded Bolt of an old arena.

"Woah." Rose gasped, looking around, her eyes large with wonder.

"What is this place?" Fury asked, looking around at all the testing dummies. He went up to one of the dummies and slashed the front of it with the spike on his tail.

"This is our training ground. It's where us guards learned how to fight." Cyclone replied with a smile. He went to one of the small rooms in the arena and pulled out a small clump of hay. "This is what we used to make those training dummies. But because we wouldn't want to waste one of them we are going to just use some hay." Cyclone added, turning to face Bolt. "Ok now I want you to try to set that pile of hay on fire."

"Um o-ok. I can try." Bolt stammered nervously, looking at the pile.

This is it. Don't mess up now or you'll look like a fool in front of everyone...again. Bolt thought nervously. Bolt focused on the pile of hay closing his eyes the same way that he focused on the fish. Except this time, instead of imagining the fire above the hay, he imagined that the fire completely engulfed the hay. When Bolt opened his eyes he let out a sigh of relief to see that the pile had caught on fire.

"Well done, I'm impressed." Cyclone observed, smiling at Bolt. "Now, I want you to try and move the fire. Try to hit that target." He said, pointing to the stone target in the distance.

What? How am I supposed to do that? Bolt thought, confused.

Just imagine the path you want the fire to move in. Whirlwind's voice said in his head.

Ok, easy, I think I can handle that. Bolt began to concentrate, his eyes locked on the flaming pile. He imagined the fire starting to lift from the ground and hover in the air. Soon, to his amazement, the fire began to float upward. Bolt let out a little gasp as it moved, which caused it to drop back into the pile.

Don't lose focus or you will lose control. Whirlwind reminded him. *Try again.*

Ok, complete focus.. Bolt thought, trying to block out everything around him. Then he looked back at the burning pile, and tried to focus on the now moving ball of fire.

Bolt moved the fire in a few curved motions, trying to get used to the feeling. Then Bolt looked directly at the target and imagined hurling the ball of fire straight at the target. The flaming ball paused, then shot forwards to the target with great speed...and missed.

Bolt let out a frustrated sigh and the amulet stopped glowing as the fire started to fade.

"That's ok. I didn't expect you to perfect it in the first try, but you definitely have made some progress." Cyclone said, congratulating Bolt. "You still have a lot to learn. But for now I want you to try something new."

Cyclone called for Storm, and Storm came speeding over to his father, carrying a bucket of water with his tail. Bolt looked over at his sister and sure enough she had that dreamy look on her face when she saw Storm.

"So how did he do?" Storm asked his father before looking at Bolt.

"He did well, but it still needs some work." Cyclone replied, grabbing the bucket of water. "Now, Bolt, today you are going to try a different element, water." He took out another pile of hay and placed it down in the middle of a circle of rocks. He then shot out a burst of lightning, catching the hay on fire. "Now, I want you to try to move that water and use it to put out the fire."

Bolt stared at the bucket of water and then looked back up at Cyclone.

How am I supposed to do that? Bolt thought with a puzzled look on his face.

Water is a bit easier to control. Imagine the water is against your scales. Then imagine that water flowing down your scales in the direction you want. Whirlwind's voice said in Bolt's head.

Oh yeah cause that's an easy thing to do Bolt thought sarcastically. Bolt closed his eyes and then tried to imagine the water flowing across his scales, moving around his body. When he opened his eyes he saw that the water was still in the bucket.

Why isn't this working!? You're not being very helpful right now. Bolt thought aggravated. *Hold on, let me try something else real quick.* Bolt closed his eyes again and then imagined the water moving and forming a little tendril, which rose out from the bucket. The amulet started glowing, but this time it was glowing with a deep blue color. When he opened his eyes, he was glad to see that the water was slowly starting to take that shape. He then pictured it forming into a small ball and the water did just that.

"There we go! Just like that." Cyclone said, looking at the small ball of water.

Bolt began to move the ball of water around in the air. He looked at Sky and gave a little smile as a small portion of the ball came off and flew at Sky, hitting her on the snout, and getting her all wet.

"Hey! Not cool!" Sky laughed, giving Bolt a silly frown.

"Come on, focus Bolt. Try to put out that fire." Cyclone said, his voice getting more serious.

"Alright, alright." Bolt muttered, regaining his focus. He aimed at the fire, and imagined throwing the ball of water at the fire. The ball flew towards the fire but stopped all of a sudden right in front of it. All of a sudden, the image of the palace fire rushed into Bolt's head.

Not this again! Bolt thought in a panic. This time though he could see Sky, dead in front of him, her body burned to a crisp. He looked around and saw the burned bodies of his friends and family all around him. *What's going on! I don't remember this happening the last time I had this dream! Did I do this?* Bolt thought, his mind being overwhelmed with feelings.

"Bolt, are you ok?" Sky asked, moving up to Bolt. "Bolt, why did you stop? Why aren't you answering me?" Bolt's eyes were glowing a deep blue, and the amulet had started glowing even brighter. Sky started shaking Bolt. "Come on Bolt. Snap out of it! Say something!" she shouted, panicking, her eyes growing wide with fear. She looked at Cyclone with a worried expression. "What's wrong with him!? What's going on!? What did you make him do!?"

The ball of water started to grow bigger and bigger, swirling around rapidly.

"I don't think he can hear you." Cyclone replied, pulling Sky away from Bolt. Sky tried to get out of his grip, but found it to be nearly impossible.

"And I didn't make him do anything that could have caused this. You remember what happened in the room with all the ice? I think whatever happened then is happening now."

"But this didn't happen the other time!" Sky shouted, her voice shaking. "Come on Bolt, you need to get control of yourself. Do something, please!" she shouted at Bolt.

This is all your fault. A new voice said in Bolt's head. *You killed them! You let them all die!* The voice hissed.

Who are you!? Why are you doing this to me!? Bolt thought, beginning to panic.

You did this to yourself. The voice hissed, seeming to come from all directions. *You let them die! You are not fit to be king! You're a nobody without a family, how could you possibly save an entire kingdom!?*

Bolt! This isn't real! There is something else in the amulet that is making you see these things so it can use your emotions to gain power and take control of you! Whirlwind shouted in Bolt's mind.

You are not a nobody. You're my son. And you do have a family. They're right beside you and they are worried about you. You have to regain control of your emotions!

The strange voice seemed to get even faster and faster, spewing out destructive words at Bolt, blocking out Whirlwind entirely. *You are worthless! You have nobody! Nobody would miss you if you were gone!*

Regain control of my emotions Bolt repeated in his head. Then, everything stopped in his mind all at once, as he could feel his heart begin to beat faster and faster, as a crackle of electricity could be heard emanating from within him.

You know what, No! Bolt thought furiously, seeming to direct his thoughts to whatever this new voice was. All of a sudden, all the hissing of the voice in his mind stopped.

What do you mean no? The voice hissed one final time, breaking the silence. Outside of his mind, Bolt's scales had started glowing a bright blue, the color of pure electricity. His tail started crackling with energy, releasing little sparks here and there.

"Everyone get behind something! Now!" Cyclone shouted. He grabbed the others and rushed to a room connected to the arena.

He opened the door and pushed everyone inside, getting in last and then he closed the door.

I am not useless! Bolt's thought furiously. *I am not alone, I have family and friends, I met the dragon I want to spend the rest of my life with. I'm not going to let whoever you are try to ruin it!* Bolt's scales started glowing even brighter, practically blinding.

I will not let you give me false feelings anymore! I will not let you warp my mind! This is my mind and you need to stay out of it! Bolt's mind shouted as he let out a deafening roar. Outside of his mind, his body had started crackling with energy, little streaks of lightning shooting out of his scales. Bolt let out one final roar as a giant burst of electricity shot out of his body in all directions. The training dummies went flying and a sound louder than thunder shook the ground. Then, everything went quiet. Cyclone slowly opened the door and gasped. There was Bolt, in the middle of the arena. He had collapsed onto the ground and he was no longer moving.

"You three stay there." Cyclone whispered, trying to keep them from seeing Bolt. But Sky pushed him out of the way and let out a loud gasp of fear. She hurried over to Bolt, tears going down her eyes.

"Come on Bolt, get up. Please Bolt, you have to get up. Don't you die on me!" she shouted, panicking, wrapping her wings around Bolt, tears streaming down her snout.

"Step aside!" Cyclone ordered, moving up to Bolt. He leaned down to Bolt's chest and let out a sigh. "It's ok, his heart is still beating."

"OK!?" Sky shouted, glaring at Cyclone. "How is this OK!? It looked like he just exploded and he isn't moving and you still call that OK!?" she hissed at him.

"What happened to him?" Rose asked, tears starting to swell up in her eyes.

"I don't know. We need to get him to a healer now." Storm announced, putting one of his wings over Rose.

"What did you do to him!" Fury hissed at Cyclone, knocking him to the ground, his tail buzzing with energy. He looked over and saw Rainstorm approaching them, her face twisted from fear. "Go get help!" He shouted at her.

"On it!" Rainstorm said, rushing to find others.

"I didn't know that would've happened. I don't have control over what the amulet does!" Cyclone confessed in a panic. Sky held on to Bolt tighter, tears still streaming down her snout. Then Sky looked at Rose with a hopeful expression.

"Can you heal him?" Sky asked Rose, her voice shaking. Rose shook her head and sighed.

"I can only heal physical injuries." Rose muttered quietly, giving Sky an apologetic look. Rainstorm hurried back, followed by a few guards. The guards gasped when they saw Bolt and hurried over.

"Come on, let's take him to the healer." Cyclone ordered, helping the guards pick up Bolt's limp body. Sky stayed there, sobbing, as they went out of view.

"It's going to be alright." Rainstorm said quietly and calmly, wrapping her wings around Sky. The four of them went to comfort Sky.

"How am I supposed to believe that?" Sky whimpered, curling up.

"Because Bolt is a survivor. He would never let a silly little necklace defeat him." Fury said, trying to speak in a soothing tone. Rainstorm looked at him with a shocked expression and then smiled.

"Fury is right. Bolt can fight through it, I know it." Rainstorm said, wrapping her tail around Fury's. Fury looked at Rainstorm and then back at Bolt, as if deep in thought. Then he broke away from the rest of the crowd with a loud roar.

"Fury wait!" Rainstorm shouted, but it was already too late, Fury had launched himself into the sky and flown away. Rainstorm looked back at Sky and let out a small sigh. She knew there was no point in chasing him, he wouldn't listen anyways. So she went back to try and comfort Sky.

"I hope you're right." Sky said, looking up at Rainstorm, tears beginning to swell up in her eyes.

"We should head over to the healer." Storm said getting up. They helped Sky get up and began heading towards the exit of the arena. As soon as they left the arena they heard thunder shake the sky as rain started to pour down from above.

CHAPTER

II

Fury's mind was racing with what had just happened, his scales beginning to glow a faint blood red as he streaked through the sky.

His mind began to swell with memories of their early childhood as he tried to hold back tears.

Why did he have to touch the stupid necklace! Everything was just starting to seem good for us, but he just had to try and be the hero. Fury thought, his mind not being able to decide whether it wanted to be angry or worried about his brother. Fury let out a roar as he shot out a massive streak of energy into the sky. He had to get out of here, even for just a moment, to catch his breath and maybe even take his anger out on some unfortunate animal that crossed his path.

With another roar he dove towards the ground, near an odd forest like area that had grown inside of the mountain. He landed with a thud as streaks of energy flew out in every direction, scorching the ground.

Poor Sky, she must be so worried about him, I've seen how she looks at him when they're together. Fury thought, a strange feeling surging through him that he hoped he would never have to feel. He shook his head, annoyed that he had begun to feel sorry for the others. But no matter how hard he tried he couldn't shake off the feeling.

Arg I'm not going to let these pathetic sappy feelings get the better of me! Fury thought, growing more and more frustrated. In his rage he lashed out at the trees surrounding him, knocking them down and scorching them with his lightning. Fury knew that this was a bad habit, but it was the only thing he knew how to do that would calm him down. Then he began to think of Rainstorm. He imagined the disappointed frown she would have given him if she saw what he was doing.

I don't know what I would do without you. He thought, taking a deep breath and closing his eyes to try and calm his nerves. He had seen Rainstorm doing this whenever she got overwhelmed, so he thought he might as well give it a try. To his amazement, all those jagged thoughts and feelings began to slowly fade away, and once everything seemed quiet, he slowly opened his eyes and looked around. He sighed, seeing what he had just done, and the smallest bit of guilt began to creep up on him.

Then he was snapped out of his calm state of mind as he heard rustling coming from behind him. He let out a hiss as he turned around, looking in the direction of the noise. There it was again, a faint rustling sound coming from an overgrown fern, as if something was moving around in it.

Perfect! Something to eat would definitely cheer me up a little, at least, for a while anyways. Fury thought, his stomach beginning to rumble.

Fury let out another hiss and rushed towards the fern, hoping to snatch whatever was hiding there before it could get away. He smiled victoriously as his tail wrapped around something in the fern, yanking it from its hiding place. Fury was hoping for a rabbit or maybe even he was lucky, a small goat, but what he saw wrapped up in his tail was this odd little creature he had never seen before.

"Now what could you be..." Fury said out loud to himself, holding the squeaking creature upside down. He brought it closer to his head and saw that it looked a little like Rose's strange monkey pet, Tiny. Except this creature didn't have fur all over its body, but just on its small little head. It also seemed to be dressed in some strange kind of fabric, and holding a small little stick.

"You are a strange little creature, oh well, you won't be around for much longer" Fury said, raising the little creature above his head as he opened his jaws. He was about to drop the unfortunate creature into his mouth when he heard more of the little squeaking coming from the fern. He stared at the fern as three more of the small little critters slowly came out of the bush, each one of them seeming to be waving their arms around at him and pointing at the one in his grasp.

Fury looked at the critter dangling above his head and then back at the others.

Are they trying to help each other? Fury thought confused and slightly curious. Annoyed, he let his curiosity get the better of him and put the little critter down, waiting to see what it would do.

The critter looked at the others by the fern, and then looked back at Fury, before running towards the others. But, right before it got back to the others, it stopped, and looked back at Fury.

"Go on, shoo, before I change my mind" Fury said, trying to shoo them off with his tail. *Why did it stop running? I let it go, so why would it want to stay around?* Fury thought, as the small little critter began to slowly walk back over to him. The others began letting out more desperate squeaks to try and get its attention. It turned back to the group, and waved its arm as if it was trying to get them to follow.

Fury watched in awe as the little critter got close enough to where it could reach out and touch his scales. He hissed again, trying to shoo it away, but it just flinched and kept getting closer. He slinked down to where his eyes met the little critters, and he could have sworn he saw the same glimmer of curiosity he had seen in Rainstorm's eyes.

Fury let out a sigh, as more memories of their time together began to wash over him. But then he thought of his brother, and he flinched instinctively. The little critter moved back a bit, but came right back up to Fury, clearly sensing his worried feelings.

The little critter sat down as if it was thinking and then quickly got up with a little squeak. It rushed over to the one of the others that seemed to be holding a small satchel of some kind. It grabbed something out of the small bag and ran back up to Fury, grabbing its small stick on the way back.

When it got close, Fury could see that it was holding some sort of scroll. *That's odd, I've never seen a scroll that small before. And how on earth did it get its hands on it?* Fury thought, as the small little critter began flipping through the pages. It stopped after a while and grabbed its stick, carving something into the ground. Fury froze as he saw what it was. It was a symbol he had read in other scrolls that when put together formed the phrase "What wrong?"

Fury shook his head, thinking that he might be seeing things, but saw that the symbol was still there, the critter looking up at him.

This is crazy, how does it know our language!? Fury thought, as he looked at the little critter with bewilderment.

Against his better judgment, he began to carve another symbol into the ground with his tail. The little critter let out a squeak as it began flipping through the book, page after page, before finally coming to a stop and looking back up at Fury with a big smile.

Fury let out a small hiss as he saw it smile. "This is serious, why are you smiling!" he said bitterly, causing the small critter to flinch back again. *Great, now I'm talking to prey.* Fury thought with a grimace.

The little critter wiped away the previous symbol and began carving out a new one. This time it read "Hurt? Have idea. Follow"

The little critter put its hand on Fury's side and went back to the others, waving its hand as if it wanted him to follow.

This is absolutely insane, I'm glad Rose isn't here or else she would never let this down. Fury thought, as he began to come closer to the group of critters. The others made high pitched squeaking sounds, clearly panicked, but began to soften as the one with the stick began squeaking back at them. It pointed to Fury as it continued to squeak at the others. The others looked at Fury as they nodded and walked off into the mossy forest ahead.

Welp, here goes nothing. Fury thought as he began to follow them through the forest.

CHAPTER

12

Fury followed them throughout the forest, surprised at how fast the little critters could go. The first one had managed to climb up onto Fury's head, and was helping him figure out which way to go. After a while, they stopped at a large mossy wall that seemed to stretch up to the top of the mountain. Fury watched as the critters on the ground ran into a small crack in the wall, disappearing from sight.

He leaned down and peered into the crevice, trying to see if there was a way he could get inside. *Now what?* Fury thought, as the critter on his head jumped down. It began flipping through the book again and started carving a symbol into the mossy ground.

"Too big. Other way. Stream"

Fury looked up, trying to see any water that might be around. Sure enough, to his left was a small river that seemed to lead into the wall. The critter pointed to the stream and then quickly followed the others into the small crack in the wall.

Very helpful. Fury thought, clearly annoyed at how unspecific the critter had been in its instructions.

Fury slinked over to the river and began to look around, trying to find this supposed "Other entrance" but didn't seem to have any luck. *What a waste of my time. I bet the critter wasn't even planning on helping me.* Fury thought bitterly.

He was about to leave when he noticed that a small fish that was swimming in the river had disappeared under the wall. He leaned in to get another look and saw that the river seemed to be flowing from inside the wall, through a large gap under the surface.

So that's what it meant... Fury thought, his mind going back to the message. He took a deep breath and dove into the water. It took a second for his eyes to get used to the rushing water as he tried to follow the current into the hole. *I hope this is the right way...* Fury thought. He would hate to drown in this river because he was following some strange creature.

Everything around him was pitch black, except for the faint glow of his scales, so he did the only thing he could do, go forward. After a few minutes of straight swimming, Fury could finally see a dim light growing in front of him. He swam towards this light, and sure enough he found himself in a large body of water, inside of the wall. He slowly swam up and saw that he was in a large cavern that had eroded overtime. And there at the other side, was the little critter that had guided him.

Woah, what is this place? He thought, as he looked around in the dimly lit cave. There were massive plants growing along the wall, each one with a strange orb in its newly budding flowers.

The little critter came up to him, and began carving into the moss.

"Home. Magic. Healing" the critter carved into the ground, looking back up at Fury. Fury stared in amazement, continuing to look around. Then one of the symbols the critter had carved got his attention. Fury pointed at the symbol for healing and looked back at the critter. But before the critter could do anything, the sound of a loud horn could be heard, coming from another crevice inside the cave.

Fury watched as dozens of the small little critters began pouring out of the crevice, each one holding a small shiny object in their hands. They all bowed as one critter stepped forth. This critter was different from the rest, as it seemed to be wearing a crown and holding a small golden staff in its hand.

It glared at Fury and then at the critter that had led him here. With a loud squeak, he pointed the staff towards the critter as the others ran forward and grabbed it. The little critter seemed to be very distressed as it tried to get away from the others, before being knocked to the ground when one of them thrust an elbow into their stomach.

What are they doing!? Fury thought, hissing at the others and trying to shoo them away from his guide.

The others pointed their strange silver objects at Fury, and he saw that they were small little swords. Seeing this, Fury laughed at the thought that they were trying to fight him.

This is gonna be easy. He thought with a sneer as he began to glow brighter, preparing to let a burst of energy wash over the strange critters. But right before he could do anything, the critter that was guiding him jumped up and got in his way with a squeak.

"What are you doing? Get out of my way so I can fry them." Fury hissed, glaring at his guide.

The little critter quickly grabbed one of the small swords and began carving another symbol in the ground.

"Family. Scared. Protective"

Fury let out an annoyed sigh as he read this. He watched as the critter put down the blade and carefully walked over to the one with the staff. They began squeaking at each other as they both gave a quick glance at Fury. The critter with the staff paused, before letting out another loud squeak as the others lowered their blades.

Then his guide pointed to one of the large flowers that was near the base of the cave and then pointed back at Fury. The other critter looked suspiciously at Fury before bringing a hand to its head with a small high pitched sigh.

His guide jumped up excitedly and rushed over to the flower. It grabbed one of the small blades and began sawing through the base of the flower, cutting it off after a few tries. Then he slowly peeled back the petals to reveal a small glowing orb inside of it.

He carefully rushed over to Fury and set it down in front of him.

What is that? Fury thought, getting a closer look at it. He Had never seen anything like it before, and he could feel a small amount of energy flowing through the orb. The little critter began to carve beside the orb.

"Healing"

Fury looked at the critter, before looking back at the orb. He carefully tucked the orb under his wing, and no sooner had it touched his scales, a rush of energy began to flow through him.

Fury turned around, and got ready to dive back into the water, but then he turned around to face the critter. He looked at all of the critters that were around him, each one giving off that same bewildered look. Then Fury began to carve into the mossy stone with his tail.

"Thank you" He muttered, looking back at his guide.

Then he turned around and dove into the water, and began his long journey back to the palace.

CHAPTER

13

It had been three days since the accident. Sky was fast asleep beside Bolt, her tail wrapped around his as she slept. Her eyes slowly opened as the healer walked into the room, followed by the rest of her friends. Rainstorm hurried over to Sky, wrapping her wings around Sky to comfort her.

"How's everything going with Bolt?" Rainstorm asked, looking at the healer. The healer grabbed something from a jar on their counter.

"There haven't been any changes. He lost a lot of energy because of the blast and we don't have a way to figure out how much energy is lost." The healer said, shaking his head and giving Sky an empathetic smile. "We haven't seen anything like this before so we have no idea if or when he will wake up."

"You mean he might never wake up?" Sky asked, her voice shaking from exhaustion and worry. She hadn't slept since the accident and she hadn't eaten anything the past few days. She just stayed at Bolt's side, waiting for something that might never come.

"Sky you need to get some sleep. You can't let yourself suffer like this." Rose insisted, trying to calm Sky down.

"Here, drink this, it should help you get some sleep." Storm insisted, pushing a small bowl filled with a strange green liquid. Sky gave a small hiss and pushed the bowl back.

"No, I can't sleep, not as long as I know that Bolt might never wake up." She replied, slowly getting up, her whole body shaking. Her body gave out as Rainstorm helped her up with her tail. She looked up as Fury came into the room. "Apparently I care more about him than his own brother." She hissed, glaring at Fury. Fury winced, hearing what Sky had said.

"I have been trying to figure out what caused him to react the way he did back at the arena." Fury replied, giving Sky a quick frown. "Unlike you, who has done nothing but sit in this room. You're basically starving yourself!"

"Sky, he's right and I think you know that. You can't just lock yourself in here for days upon days." Rainstorm added, looking at Sky with a little smile. Then she grabbed the bowl and brought it back. "Staying here and torturing yourself is not going to help Bolt. You need to get some rest and eat something, that's what Bolt would want you to do, isn't it?" she insisted, pushing the bowl back to Sky. Sky looked down and the bowl and let out a long exhausted sigh. She nodded her head and looked back up at Rainstorm.

"No, he wouldn't want me to suffer like this." Sky confessed, her voice quiet and worn out from exhaustion. Sky looked back at the bowl with a frown. She quickly drank the contents and pushed the bowl aside with a sigh. Rainstorm gave her a quick hug as everyone else began to leave the room.

"That should help you get to sleep." Rainstorm whispered to Sky in a calm tone.

"He's going to be ok, I know it." She gave Sky another quick hug and left the room. Sky sighed and laid back down, her eyelids starting to droop.

"He's gonna be ok, everything is going to be ok." Sky said quietly as her eyes began to close and she fell asleep. She dreamed that she was flying beside Bolt, high in the sky where nobody could hurt them. Then all of a sudden that dream started to fade and she found herself in the frozen chamber. Sky shivered and looked around, confused about what was going on.

How did I get here? Wasn't I just flying in the sky with Bolt? She said, confused. She looked at Snowstorm, still frozen in the block of ice. A little clatter came from the stairs of the chamber. Sky turned around and gasped, there was a wall of ice where the stairs should have been. *How is this possible? What's going on?* She muttered, rubbing her eyes making sure that it was really there.

Simple, you're dreaming, and unfortunately for you it's not a good one. A voice hissed at her. Sky quickly turned around and saw Snowstorm right in front of her, the block of ice containing her seeming to have disappeared. Sky let out a little scream and backed up against the wall, her eyes locked onto the fuming dragon.

What do you mean I'm dreaming! How is this possible!? You're not dead so how are you speaking to me!? Sky asked, her voice shaking with fear.

I have other ways to get into the minds of others. Snowstorm snarled.

And thanks to that "hero" of a son, I was woken and I saw what had happened to me.

Sky let gasped as the room around her started to change again. The ice surrounding the walls had melted away and there was blood everywhere. She looked down and yelped, seeing the corpse of a guard laying on the ground.

How did you get out!? Sky shouted in fear. She looked at Snowstorm's expression and immediately answered her own question. *You didn't get out did you?* She asked, letting out a thankful sigh.

I have almost freed myself from this frozen cell. Snowstorm hissed, giving Sky a wicked smile. *I'll already be free before you can even get back to the chamber.*

Sky's eyes snapped open as she woke up in a panic. She looked around, making sure she was back in the healers room. Sky let out a long sigh as she looked down at Bolt. Tears began to flow down her snout as she put her wings around Bolt.

"Why won't you just wake up. We need you to wake up, I have a feeling something horrible is going to happen." She whispered, closing her eyes and wiping away her tears. She jumped, startled, as the healer came rushing into the room and shouting. He was carrying something that Sky had never seen before. It looked like a large glowing orb, the same color as Bolt's glowing scales.

"Sorry but I'm going to need you to move aside!" the healer announced, moving Sky to the side. The healer grabbed the orb and shot a small bolt of lightning from his mouth into the orb.

"What are you doing?" Sky asked, confused by what was going on. She tried to move closer to Bolt but the healer kept pushing her away. Sky jumped again as another voice came from the entry of the room.

"It's a static orb, it should give Bolt just enough energy to be able to wake him up." Fury interjected, moving up towards Sky. "I was able to find one in the mountain. They're very rare and I was lucky enough to have found one while I was exploring."

"You really looked through the entire mountain just to find it?" Sky asked, the tears starting to come back into her eyes. She saw Rainstorm and Rose rush into the room.

"Yep, I spent days trying to find something to help Bolt and I learned about these things called static orbs." Fury replied, a smile starting to spread across his face. Rainstorm gave him a big hug and looked him in the eyes.

"I knew you had some good in you!" Rainstorm shouted with joy. She pulled Fury into another long hug before letting go and moving over to where Bolt was laying. Sky looked at the healer with a hopeful smile.

"So you're sure this will wake him up?" Sky managed to choke out. The healer nodded his head and smiled. He brought the orb to his desk and dropped it into a glass of water. The orb dissolved instantly and the water gave off a slight glow. He slowly opened Bolt's mouth and poured the liquid into his mouth and made him swallow.

"He should be awake in a couple hours." The healer added, smiling at the group.

"Do you mind giving us a moment?" Sky asked the healer. He nodded and left the room, closing the door behind him. Sky then quickly turned around to the others, her face now giving off a worried expression.

"What's wrong?" Rose asked Sky, seeing her expression. "Shouldn't you be happy about this?"

"I am happy, extremely happy. But I don't think we can wait a couple hours." Sky said, the worried expression only seeming to get stronger. "Last night I was having a normal dream and then I just appeared in the chamber where Snowstorm is kept. And then Snowstorm spoke to me in my dream somehow, she said she's going to escape soon!" Sky confessed. All of a sudden the room went completely silent as the others just stared at Sky in shock.

"How soon?" Storm asked in a serious tone. "I need to know so I can go warn my father." Sky shook her head and sighed.

"There is no point, we were too late when we tried to stop Bolt down in the chamber, Snowstorm said she would be free before we even got back to the chamber." Sky confessed.

"We still need to warn everyone!" Rose shouted, hurrying out of the door. Storm was about to follow her but looked back at the group.

"Rainstorm, you stay here with Sky for when Bolt wakes up, Fury, you come with me and Rose to go and warn everyone." Fury nodded his head and followed Storm out of the room. Rainstorm looked at Sky as the others flew off to find Cyclone.

"Is it really too late?" Rainstorm asked Sky. "Are you sure you didn't get anything wrong?" Sky shook her head and looked at Bolt, tears starting to roll down her snout.

"Yes, I know what I heard. Bolt is going to be so upset when he hears this." Sky muttered, her tail wrapping around Bolt's tail. Bolt's tail was now giving off a faint glow as the energy orb started to give him energy. Sky let go of his tail with a gasp, Bolt's wings shuttered and he slowly opened his eyes.

"Sky?" Bolt said quietly, in the same tone of voice Sky had used earlier that day.

"You're awake!" Sky shouted, quickly pulling Bolt into a long hug. "The healer was right! You have no idea how long I've been waiting for this." She confessed, tears streaming down her cheeks as she hugged him tighter. Bolt's eyes opened a bit more and he looked around confused. He slowly raised his head and looked at Sky.

"What are you talking about? Where am I? What's going on?" Bolt asked, looking at Rainstorm and then looking back at Sky.

"There was an accident and you lost a lot of your energy because of that stupid amulet. You've been unconscious for three days. We thought you were never going to wake up." Sky stammered, her voice shaking as tears continued to roll down her cheeks. "But Fury found this strange orb that was able to give you just enough energy to wake you up." Bolt looked surprised hearing that last part.

"You mean my brother helped me? That's not something I thought he would ever do." Bolt said, bewildered. "But at least I'm ok, now you don't have to worry about me anymore." He added, smiling at Sky and wiping away her tears. "Was I really out for three days?" He asked, looking at Rainstorm. Rainstorm nodded and moved up beside him and Sky.

"Yeah, and Sky has been spending a lot of time in this room waiting for you to wake up. She would have starved herself if it wasn't for us." Rainstorm replied, smiling at the two of them.

Rose, Storm, and Fury rushed into the room with Cyclone right behind them. They immediately saw Bolt and rushed over to his side.

"You're awake!' Rose shouted, running into Bolt at full speed and gave him a tight hug. Fury just let out a little snort as he came up beside Bolt.

"Oh don't act like you aren't happy, Sky told me what you did." Bolt smirked, giving his brother a hug. Fury started to pull out but stopped and smiled.

"Fine, so I might have cared if my brother ended up dying." Fury replied, Sky then looked at Fury with a confused expression.

"What do you mean dying?" Sky asked. "He wouldn't have died, he just wouldn't have woken up." Sky looked at the nervous expression on Fury's face and glared at him. "What did you do?" she hissed at him.

"Oh nothing." Fury replied quickly. "I'm hungry, is anyone else hungry? I'll go get us something to eat." He hurried towards the exit but Rainstorm moved in front of him blocking his path.

"You're not getting out of this one that easily. I believe Sky asked you a question." Rainstorm said in an annoyed voice. She turned Fury around to where he was facing Sky.

"Ok so I might have forgotten to mention that the energy orb only had a slight chance at working, and if it didn't work it would have killed him." Fury confessed, his eyes darting around nervously.

"What!" Sky roared at him. She slapped him across the face with her tail and glared at him. "I can't believe you did that! You should have found something that was sure to work, not something that could have killed him!" Rainstorm quickly went in front of Fury, keeping Sky from attacking him again.

"Now now, we all know that what Fury did probably wasn't the smartest thing to do. But Sky, it worked, so you need to calm down and apologize to Fury." Rainstorm interjected, trying to calm Sky down.

"You want me to apologize!?" Sky hissed. "But he-"

"Apologize." Rainstorm said sternly, refusing to back down. "Now." Sky took a deep breath and let out a long sigh. "See, much better. Now apologize." Rainstorm said with a smile. She moved out of the way so Sky could speak to Fury.

"I'm sorry I attacked you, It wasn't the right thing to do." Sky muttered sourly. Fury rubbed his aching snout and glared at Sky, then gave her a little smile.

"Apology accepted, we all do the wrong thing from time to time." He replied.

"Fury, thank you for not acting irrationally to what Sky did." Rainstorm added, looking at Fury with a smile.

"Well now that that's over with, I think we should let Bolt know of our current problem." Storm insisted, moving over to Bolt. Bolt looked at him with a confused expression. "Bolt, you remember back in the chamber when you had your first little problem with the amulet?" Storm asked him with a serious expression.

"Yeah, what about it?" Bolt replied, still confused about what was going on.

"Well apparently we were too late and you sort of woke up Snowstorm and she escaped." Storm added quickly, waiting for

Bolt's response. Bolt immediately got up with a fierce look in his eyes.

"She escaped!? How did she escape!? When did you find out!?" Bolt demanded, his eyes filled with rage. Cyclone went up to Bolt to try and calm him down.

"Bolt, remember, control your emotions. You don't want the amulet to try and feed off of your anger." He said, reaching out for Bolt. Bolt waved him away and gave a triumphant smile.

"I don't have to worry about that anymore." Bolt replied, his smile seeming to get even bigger. "I was able to stop the amulet from feeding off of my emotions and making me feel even stronger emotions." Cyclone looked at Bolt with a shocked expression.

"I would ask how but I do believe we have more important matters at hand." Cyclone observed, looking directly at Bolt. "We will have to send a search party to try and find Snowstorm, but for now we have to get you to the desert border as soon as possible to speak with King Scorpius. He is already annoyed by the fact you weren't able to come earlier due to what happened."

"But I'm not ready!" Bolt stammered, his eyes growing wide. "I barely got any practice with the amulet, what if something happens!?"

"Then we are just going to have to hope for the best." Cyclone replied. "We don't have much of a choice now."

CHAPTER

14

"What am I gonna do, what am I gonna do, what am I gonna do!?" Bolt thought, his mind buzzing with worry and fear as the desert border came into view. "I barely survived using my amulet last time so how could I possibly stop a fight with it now!?"

Sky looked over and saw the nervous expression on Bolt's face and flew up beside him.

"Everything alright?" she asked him, giving him a worried smile. "I know you might be nervous, I am too, but I am absolutely positive that nothing could go wrong here." Sky looked at Bolt with a smile that made him feel all warm inside. "I'm sure as long as we stick together we will all come out of this completely unharmed." Sky added.

"Welp that settles it, we're all going to die." Fury muttered. "I hope everyone had a good life until now." Bolt's nervous expression only seemed to grow when he heard his brother say that. Sky looked over at Fury and glared at him.

"Must you always be so negative!?" Sky hissed. "If you couldn't tell I'm trying to get Bolt to stop worrying and *you're* not helping by saying that we are all going to die!" Rainstorm nudged Fury and looked at him with an amused expression.

"Why are you so tense all of a sudden?" Rainstorm asked, giving Fury a little smile. "You're the 'great and powerful Fury', what could you possibly be worried about?" she said sarcastically. Fury snorted and rolled his eyes, turning his head to look at Rainstorm.

"I'm not worried about me, I'm going to be perfectly fine. It's just that for example you don't have as good of a chance of surviving as I do and I would hate to lose a member of the team." Fury replied with a snort. Rainstorm laughed and smiled at Fury.

"Awww is someone worried about me? That is sooo sweet of you. You're such a sweetheart, you know that right?" Rainstorm teased. Bolt couldn't keep himself from laughing after hearing what Rainstorm had said. Fury glared at his brother before looking back at Rainstorm.

"I am *not* a sweetheart!" he hissed. "I am a warrior, an unstoppable force that casts fear into the hearts of all who oppose me!" Rainstorm let out another laugh, after a while, she eventually was able to regain herself before looking at Fury with a smile.

"Of course you are. I bet everyone there is already trembling in fear at the border." She teased. Fury looked back, hearing Rose burst into laughter, he scowled and looked ahead of him towards the border. Everyone slowly came to a stop as Storm came up to the border. Two guards were stationed there both holding spears and giving off menacing expressions.

"State your business here." One of the guards ordered, blocking the entry of the border. Storm let out a sigh and looked back up at the guards.

"We're here for the meeting with King Scorpius." Storm replied, moving aside so they could see Bolt.

"Very well then." The other guard said. The two guards lowered their spears and let the six of them enter. Storm led them into the meeting room and turned to Bolt with an apologetic look.

"I know you're a bit nervous and this probably won't help much, but I will not be able to stay here when you meet King Scorpius. I have to go help my father track down Snowstorm." Storm announced, looking at the group. Rose looked at him with a frown.

"But what if something goes wrong?" Rose asked him, giving him a worried look.

"The guards outside will rush in and help as much as they can if anything bad does happen." Storm replied. "And Bolt has his amulet, so you should be fine." Bolt looked at Storm with a concerned frown.

"But I barely know how to control this thing!" Bolt replied, his voice shaking. Hearing Bolt's discomfort, Sky moved up beside him and wrapped her tail around his, trying to calm him down. She turned to face him, giving him a big smile.

"It's going to be ok. Remember, as long as we have each other nothing can go wrong. And even if something does happen, we will fight against it, together." She said in a soothing voice. Bolt gave her a little smile and turned back to face the group.

"She's right, as long as we have each other we can face any obstacle, as a team." Bolt announced, looking at each and every one of them. His motivational speech would have worked, but then the ground started to shake as loud footsteps could be heard. Everyone turned around, facing the desert and saw what was approaching. It was King Scorpius, a massive scorpion, much bigger than the dune scorpion Bolt fought when he first met Sky. And this one had not one but three massive tails each with a razor sharp barb on the end. King Scorpius made his way to the border glaring right at Bolt.

"I see that the so-called lost heir has finally decided to show his face." King Scorpius hissed, all eight of his beady eyes locked onto Bolt. Then he looked at the amulet that was around Bolt's neck and smiled. "It seems that the king was too scared to come without bringing his little toy." Bolt hissed, glaring at King Scorpius.

"I am not scared!" Bolt hissed, staring directly at Scorpius. "And I will fight if I have to." Scorpius let out a little chuckle, looking at the group that was with Bolt.

"Fighting would be a fatal mistake, little dragon. You could not possibly beat me." Scorpius sneered, the barbs on his tails gleaming with venom.

"Now now, we didn't come here for a fight." Sky assured, giving Bolt a quick glance. "The only reason why we are here is because you wanted to meet the future king." She added with a smile.

"But just to be clear, they might not be willing to fight, but I am not like them." Fury pointed out, before being silenced by Sky's annoyed glare. Scorpius let out a deep laugh, before speaking up.

"I admire this ones bravery, are you any way interested in working for me?" He said with a snarl. Before Fury could say anything, Rainstorm spoke up, glaring at Scorpius.

"No! He's not going to work for you. He wouldn't even dare to think about that!" she hissed, glancing back at Fury with a hopeful expression. Fury seemed shocked by the fact that she was doing this for him.

"Well that's a shame…You can't have them all." Scorpius said in a deep monotone voice.

"Can we just get on with this? Why did you want to meet with me?" Bolt demanded, his patience wearing thin. *Why does he seem to be avoiding the question? Is he stalling for something? What if this is all a trap and he's just waiting for his soldiers to arrive?* Bolt thought in a panic.

Relax, I've known Scorpius for quite some time, he is not clever enough to make a plan like that. Whirlwind said in Bolt's mind, trying to comfort him. Bolt continued to think of this until he heard Sky say something.

"So, Bolt, is this alright with you?" Sky asked, facing him. Bolt blinked, completely confused. He looked around and saw everyone looking at him.

"Well? I don't have all day." Scorpius sneered, all eight of his beady eyes staring him down. Bolt frantically looked at his friends before stopping at Sky with a worried expression.

"Is everything alright?" Sky asked, beginning to grow worried.

"I was worrying so much about what this meeting could be. I completely missed what Scorpius had said!" Bolt replied in a hushed voice.

"He wants us to share the jungle with him in return for protection against any future threats." Sky replied, keeping her voice down.

Now this, this is a trap. Whirlwind's voice exclaimed.

What are you talking about? Bolt replied

Scorpius has been trying to persuade us to give him the jungle in return for protection but we found out he would try to overthrow us afterwards. Whirlwind said. Bolt then took a deep breath to calm himself down and went forward.

"Your request is denied." He managed to choke out, quickly moving back. Scorpius glared at him, his pinchers snapping open and closed.

"Well then...that's a shame. I was hoping you would be more reasonable than your father." He sneered. "But just in case you haven't noticed, your kingdom is dying. That jungle will be mine, with or without your approval."

"So what if our kingdom is dying, I will still fight for my kingdom's needs as long as there is still air in my lungs." Bolt hissed, the amulet beginning to glow a faint red.

"We'll see about that." Scorpius hissed, eyeing the amulet. Then without warning he stormed out of the room.

"Well that went well." Rainstorm said nervously, glancing around the room.

"What part of that seemed well to you?" Bolt asked, clearly annoyed.

"I'm just glad you stood up against him." Sky said with a smile, her tail beginning to wrap around his. All of a sudden Storm burst into the room, a deep cut along his side bleeding rapidly. Rose gasped and rushed over to Storm, her face twisted with panic.

"What happened to you!?" she asked in a panic, quickly placing her tail on the wound. Storm winced as she did this, but began to calm down as the pinkish energy traveled around the wound. His eyes widened as he saw this, he looked up at Rose and the others with confusion?

"Oh yeah did we forget to mention that our sister can heal others?" Fury said with a smirk. Rainstorm nudged him with her wing and glared at him.

"Now is not the time for your antics." She said in a stern voice.

"Well, what happened?" Rose repeated, as she finished healing the cut on Storm's side. Storm took a deep breath and began to explain to them what had happened.

"We had managed to catch up with Snowstorm at the frozen tundra, in a little string of tunnels under the ice. We thought that we had cornered her, but we had no idea how wrong we were.

"She must have known we were coming, and before we knew it we were being ambushed. Spikes of ice began rapidly forming in the tunnels blocking the way out.

"Then she attacked us, picking us off one by one. My father tried to stop her but she killed him. I only escaped because I was able to squeeze through the spikes." Storm managed to choke out in between sobs.

"That's awful!" Rose muttered, pulling Storm into a hug. "But you're safe with us now, and we will do everything we can to bring Snowstorm to justice."

"Come on, let's head back to the palace. I will make sure that Cyclone will not have died in vain." Bolt added, helping Storm up.

I can't believe she killed Cyclone, I promise you Storm, not only will I find Snowstorm, but I will kill her for what she has done to us. Bolt thought, eyes tearing up from grief and hatred. He looked down at the amulet that hung around his neck.

And I will do whatever it takes to make it happen.

CHAPTER

15

When they arrived back at the palace everyone gathered around, looking at the group with anticipation. They could tell something was wrong, slowly starting to worry. Bolt let out a long sigh before looking out at the crowd. Rose was helping Storm inside, keeping a wing around him. Bolt looked as they disappeared into the palace and then looked back at the gathering crowd.

I guess it is finally time for them to know what is going on. Bolt thought, before clearing his throat.

"Now I know all of you might be wondering why there was a group of guards leaving the kingdom yesterday." Bolt said, making a slight pause before continuing. "A couple of nights ago our kingdom's biggest threat was re-awakened, Snowstorm managed to escape from her icy prison. Those guards were sent to track her down and stop her by any means necessary.

"Unfortunately, they were ambushed and killed after stopping in the frozen tundra." The crowd around them let out a gasp, hearing the news.

"Did they at least find her?" someone in the crowd asked.

"Even if they did, she is long gone by now." Bolt said with a sigh. "And because of these events I have made the decision that our kingdom is going to need a king, but all you've got is me. I know that I might not be the bravest of the bunch, but it is my duty as prince, son of Whirlwind, that I am finally taking my place on the throne." Fury's head snapped up when he heard this. He gave a slight hiss and stormed away from the group. Rainstorm gave Bolt a worried look, before looking back in the direction that Fury was going.

"You should go. If any of us could calm him down it would be you." Bolt whispered, giving Rainstorm a small smile before looking back at the crowd. Rainstorm nodded and went off to follow Fury.

"And it is hard for me to say this but I believe we need to put this kingdom on lockdown, nobody comes in or out without my permission. I know this might stress you out but it is the best option for us until Snowstorm is brought down. You are dismissed."

Sky looked at Bolt with a worried expression.

"Are you sure this is a good idea? This could keep us from getting to the resources we need to survive." She whispered. "And what are we supposed to do until then?"

"For now we will spend this time mourning the deceased." Bolt responded. "But come tomorrow I will be going out to find anyone who will be willing to help us."

"Alone!? Are you insane! What if Snowstorm comes after you?" Sky hissed.

"Then I will fight until one of us is dead." Bolt replied.

"No way, we are coming with you!" Sky said with a slight hiss. "And there is no way you can talk your way out of this one."

"No way! You heard what she did to the guards." Bolt replied.

"Which is exactly why you can't go alone." Sky sighed, looking at Bolt with worried eyes. "Our kingdom already lost one king to her, we won't let it lose another, I won't let it lose another." She added, pulling him into a tight hug. Bolt's heart practically screamed out for her when she did this, his stare softening.

"Fine." Bolt gave in with a sigh. "Now, let's go see if we can find where my brother stormed off to." The two of them went off in the direction where both Rainstorm and Fury had gone, Bolt's mind buzzing with what was going on. Images of his first dream appeared in his head, seeming to become more and more detailed.

This is all my fault. If I hadn't caused the ice to melt Snowstorm wouldn't have been able to break free. And if she never broke free she wouldn't have been able to kill all those guards, including Storm's father. Am I the reason our kingdom gets destroyed? He thought, tears beginning to roll down his cheeks. Sky looked over at him and gave him a small smile.

"Is everything alright?" she asked, staring directly into his eyes.

"No, ever since I got here I've done nothing right. Everything I touch seems to go up in flames. I'm starting to believe there is nothing I can do to help anymore." Bolt muttered.

"Don't say that, you've been doing a great job. And not everything you've touched went up in flames. Look around, you've got friends here, others who would put their life on the line for you. And you've got me, and I will always stick by your side." Sky said with a smile, wiping away Bolt's tears. Bolt smiled as they continued looking for the others. It wasn't hard to track down Fury, considering the trail of seared cuts in the stone around them. After a while the cuts ended as they turned into a little tunnel that seemed to go on for quite a while.

"You think they went in there?" Sky asked, looking at Bolt.

"Only one way to find out." Bolt replied, heading into the tunnel. The tunnel seemed to get tighter and tighter as they continued, barely large enough for them to fit. Soon only one of them would be able to continue on.

"I'll go first, just in case there is anything dangerous on the other side." Bolt insisted.

"Oh don't be silly, that would never happen, I'll go first." Sky replied, moving forward before Bolt could respond. She continued going forward until Bolt could no longer see her.

"Sky? Sky, are you there? Is everything alright?" Bolt shouted, worried that something might have happened.

"Yeah I'm here. But you have got to get over here and see this." Sky responded.

After a slight pause Bolt began to move further until he reached a little opening. He gasped as he looked at the astonishing reflective cave walls that surrounded them. There was a small lake of water that filled the bottom of the cave, except for the singular small island in the middle of the lake. Bolt crawled out of the tunnel and looked around in amazement, before looking at Sky.

"What is this place?" he asked, getting a closer look at the cave walls.

"I have no idea. I've never seen anything like this before. And to think something like this was hidden in our kingdom." Sky replied in wonder. She stopped as the two of them heard voices coming from the little island.

"Could that be them?" she asked, trying to spot any sort of movement on the island.

"I don't know, let's go find out." Bolt replied, going into the water. To his surprise, the water seemed to give off a faint glow when he moved around. Sky nervously looked at him and then looked up at the cave ceiling.

"Couldn't we just fly there?" she asked nervously.

"I don't think so, the ceiling seems too low for us to fly." Bolt replied, giving Sky a confused look.

"Then I might just stay here while you go check it out." Sky insisted, backing away from the water.

"Don't be ridiculous, we should both go and check it out. Don't tell me you're afraid of a little water?" Bolt snickered, splashing water at Sky.

"I am not!" Sky replied quickly before backing away again. "I just don't know how to swim." She muttered quietly. Bolt laughed and after a while he stopped when he saw her face.

"Wait, you're being serious? You don't know how to swim?" Bolt asked, a small frown spreading across his snout. Sky shook her head and looked away with embarrassment. Bolt got out of the water and went up to her.

"Why didn't you tell me sooner?" he asked.

"Well I don't normally introduce myself by saying 'Hi I'm Sky and I can't swim.' because that would be embarrassing." Sky muttered, wrapping her wings around herself.

"It's not that hard, I can teach you." Bolt insisted, giving Sky a small smile.

"I really don't think that's necessary." Sky started, letting out a little yelp as Bolt tugged her into the water.

"What are you doing!?" she stuttered, coughing up a bit of water. She began to thrash around trying to get back to the rocky ledge she had been on.

"Relax, you don't have to worry I've got you." Bolt said with a smile, turning her to where she was facing him. Sky stopped and took a deep breath, trying to calm down.

"A little warning would have been nice though." She muttered sourly.

"Now it's just like flying, angle your wings in the direction you want to go." Bolt said calmly. Sky tried to do what Bolt had said and looked back at him. "Now use your tail to make yourself go forward." Bolt added. Sky followed his instructions and found herself going forward, with Bolt right beside her.

"I'm doing it! I'm actually doing it!" Sky exclaimed, a smile beaming on her face.

"See, it wasn't that hard now was it?" Bolt said with a smile. Sky looked at him with that same bright smile, making Bolt's heart beat faster. The two continued to stare at each other, seemingly entranced by one another, before Sky finally spoke up.

"Do you think everything is going to be ok?" she murmured in a hushed voice. "Everything has been going wrong lately, I'm worried that it's only a matter of time before something happens to one of us."

Bolt gave her a small smile.

"I know things might seem bad, but you remember when we first met? It seemed like things couldn't get any worse for you. But then I showed up and gave you hope."

Bolt lifted her chin up with his tail. "I protected you then, and I will protect you now until the day we must join our ancestors in the heavens."

Sky smiled and pulled Bolt into a tight hug. They stayed there, floating in the water, wings locked together for what felt like hours. Eventually they got themselves together and started swimming towards the small island where they hoped to find Fury.

When they eventually reached the island they found Fury laying in the middle of what appeared to be a small circle of glowing flowers and stones. Fury raised his head and opened his eyes, hearing the two approach him.

"How did you find me?" Fury asked, his voice unusually calm, his eerie red glow seeming to have changed to a beautiful ruby red. Bolt and Sky stopped beside him, a look of confusion and curiosity on their faces.

"It wasn't too hard to find you. You kind of left a trail of slash marks on the walls."

Bolt explained, a small smile spreading across his face.

"What is this place?" Sky asked, looking at Fury with a look of extreme curiosity. She slid her tail through a group of flowers that were giving off a dim purple glow. There was a moment of silence before Fury let out a sigh and began to explain.

"You remember that orb I found to heal Bolt?" He asked, looking back and forth between the two of them. Sky gave a small nod, giving a quick glance at Bolt.

"Yeah, what about it?" she asked.

"This is where I found it." Fury replied. "I came across this place after we left your home after chasing after a small boar that had wandered inside. I lost it at this lake and then I saw something glowing bright like the sun coming from the middle of the lake.

"I swam across and found this island and saw the orb sticking out of the ground in a group of glowing stones. All the color and light felt somewhat comforting, so I've been coming here every night since then."

Bolt and Sky just stared at him with amusement.

"Why didn't you tell us about this place?" Bolt asked, dipping his tail into the water, watching as it began to glow.

"Because I didn't want anyone to know about this place, I just wanted a place where I can go to calm down, away from any distractions." Fury replied with a sigh.

"Promise me you won't tell anyone about this place." He added, a serious expression falling upon his snout.

"We promise." Sky said with a smile, putting one of her wings around him.

The three of them just sat there for some time, staring at the shining cave walls before Bolt finally got up.

"We should probably head back now, Rainstorm has been looking for you and you wouldn't want to worry her." Bolt announced, before heading towards the water. Fury and Sky did the same not long after. They had almost made it to the other side when Bolt suddenly stopped. Sky turned around and gave him a puzzled look.

"Why did you stop?" she asked, before noticing the dark blue glow that was beginning to radiate from the amulet around Bolts neck. She let out a small gasp, staring at Bolt, her eyes filled with fear and worry. Hearing this Fury turned around and saw what was going on.

"Not this again." Fury said in an aggravated tone. " Sky we should probably go now." He added, rushing over to Sky. Sky just continued to stare at Bolt, unable to utter a single word.

This can't be happening. Sky thought in a panic, *I can't let him hurt himself again. What if he doesn't make it this time.*

Then right before Fury could get to her she began to swim to Bolt. When she reached him she wrapped her wings around him, holding him tight, tears beginning to form in your eyes.

"Sky don't!" Fury shouted, beginning to race over to the two of them, before a wall of water burst out from under him. Fury let out a gasp as he watched the wall go over Bolt and Sky. He closed his eyes as it rushed down at them, waiting for the crash of the wave hitting them, but the crash never came. He slowly opened his eyes and his jaw dropped as he saw that the water had formed a large sphere around Bolt and Sky.

Sky looked around in fear and wonder at the sphere that had surrounded her and Bolt. Then she looked back at Bolt and saw that his eyes were shut tight, not glowing like they were in the arena. After a while she tried to regain herself and leaned in, her head beside his.

"Bolt, I'm here, you're alright. I know that you're scared and that's ok. But I want you to know that I will be here for you the entire time." She whispered to Bolt, resting her head against his. It went silent for a moment before Bolt let out a sigh.

"But what if when I open my eyes I see that I've hurt someone?" He asked, his voice shaking.

"Then we will deal with that together, but we won't have to because you aren't going to hurt anybody." Sky replied in a hushed tone. Bolt let out another sigh before slowly opening his eyes. He stared in wonder at the sphere of water that was surrounding them. Then he looked at Sky, and all the worry slowly began to fade away as a small smile spread across his face. He wrapped his wings around her and held her tight.

"You were willing to give your life to try and help me." Bolt stuttered, letting her go.

"I didn't want to risk losing you for good this time." Sky replied, giving him a small smile.

"Yeah yeah yeah, you like each other, we get it. Now can you please focus on trying to figure out what is going on!?" Fury shouted, looking around and trying to find a way past the walls of water.

Sky shot a dangerous glare towards Fury for interrupting their moment.

"That's probably a good idea." Bolt said nervously. "Only problem, I have no idea how to do that."

"Well you're the one that's controlling it, so just do the opposite of what you're doing right now." Fury replied. Bolt looked down at the amulet which was still glowing a deep blue.

I don't know how I did this, how am I going to undo it? Bolt thought worriedly.

Don't ask me, it seems that the amulet works differently for you than for me. Whirlwinds voice said in Bolts head.

Maybe if I calm my nerves I might be able to get better control. Bolt thought hopefully. Bolt took a deep breath and closed his eyes, trying to put his mind and body at ease. He imagined the sphere of water slowly beginning to open up. When he opened his eyes he saw that the water had split forming a small exit.

It's working! Bolt thought with excitement.

"Come on Bolt you've got this, you just need to make the exit a little bit bigger." Sky said with a smile. Hearing her support, Bolt gave her a quick smile,before focusing back on the exit. The split in the water slowly grew larger and larger until it was big enough for them to go through. They quickly swam out and hurried over to Fury. When they reached him they all stared back at the sphere of water, which had closed back up.

Bolt took another deep breath and closed his eyes. After a while the sphere of water began to split at the top and slowly flowed back down. Bolt opened his eyes and let out a sigh of relief, the glow of the amulet slowly fading away.

"Ok thankfully that's over with. I think now would be a good time to leave." Fury said, quickly hurrying over to the tunnel.

"Now that's the first thing you've said that I agree with." Sky said with a little snicker. Fury rolled his eyes, but quickly turned away from them, trying to hide a small smile. The three of them followed the tunnel back to kingdom, Bolt peeking his head out first to make sure nobody was around. Then they began to head back to the palace where the others were waiting for them.

CHAPTER

16

here are they? Rainstorm thought nervously, pacing back and forth. *It's been hours since they went looking for Fury. I hope nothing happened to them.*

"Are you doing ok?" Rose asked, moving up to Rainstorm. Rainstorm jumped, not having heard Rose approach. She took a deep breath to regain herself and turned to face Rose.

"No, not really. I'm beginning to worry that something has happened to the others." She replied with a sigh, her head hanging low.

"Oh I'm sure everything is fine, Bolt wouldn't let anything happen to Sky." Rose snickered, coiling up beside Rainstorm. She stopped when she saw how serious Rainstorms expression was.

"It's not Bolt I'm worried about." Rainstorm muttered, shaking her head.

"Oh you're talking about Fury, aren't you?" Rose asked, looking up at Rainstorm. Rainstorm gave a small little nod, closing her eyes.

"I don't want him to get into any trouble." Rainstorm sighed, slowly opening her eyes, tears beginning to build in her eyes.

"I wouldn't be too worried, we both know what he could do if anything happened to him." Rose pointed out, trying to make Rainstorm feel better.

"That's exactly what I'm worried about. I've been trying so hard to keep him from doing anything that could get him into a lot of trouble.

"I'm just worried that if something does happen, there won't be anything I can do to stop him." Rainstorm sighed, tears beginning to roll down her snout. Rose looked at her with an empathetic smile. She spread one of her wings around Rainstorm, doing as much as she could to make her feel better.

"You must really like him." Rose said with a smile. "If you're willing to do so much to try and help him." Rainstorm looked down at Rose, giving her a small thankful smile.

"I do, I'm just worried it will only be a matter of time until something pushes him too far away for me to be able to help." Rainstorm muttered, wiping away her tears.

"How about we talk some more about this later? Storm is making something for us to eat, I wouldn't want to let him down, especially not after what happened to his father." Rose said with a smile, slowly beginning to get up.

"I didn't know he could cook." Rainstorm said with a smile, following right behind Rose, the two of them beginning to head towards the dining hall. Rainstorm looked back at the entrance one final time. *Fury, wherever you are, please stay safe.* She thought before turning back again.

As the two of them got closer to the dining hall entrance they were hit by a wave of wonderful aromas. They could smell all sorts of different foods coming from the dining hall. When they went in they were met with a very excited looking Storm, with a goofy grin on his face.

"I knew you two would come." Storm said, wrapping his wings around them before bringing them to the table.

"Wow! You made all this?" Rose gasped.

"Yep, well most of it. I had some help from the other chefs." Storm replied, his face beginning to turn a light shade of red, quickly turning away from them. Rainstorm nudged Rose with her wing when Storm looked away. Rose looked at Rainstorm, who had a little smile on her face.

"I think someone is warming up to you." Rainstorm whispered to Rose.

"Do you really think so?" Rose whispered back in a half excited, half nervous voice. She quickly got quiet as Storm turned back around.

"Well, I believe everything is ready now, so we can start eating." Storm said with a smile.

"Shouldn't we wait for the others?" Rose asked with a frown.

"No, we should just go ahead and eat. I have a feeling it will be some time before they return." Rainstorm sighed, shaking her head.

"Oh, ok." Rose muttered, looking at Rainstorm with a worried expression.

The three of them gathered around the table and watched as the food was passed around. Both Storm and Rose had begun eating and after a while they stopped, noticing that Rainstorm hadn't eaten anything.

"You ok? Do you not like the food?" Storm asked, a puzzled look on his face.

"No, the food looks wonderful. I just don't have much of an appetite right now." Rainstorm said with a sigh.

How can I eat knowing that the others could be in trouble right now. Rainstorm thought, a frown beginning to form on her face. Storm gave Rainstorm a worried look, before looking at Rose.

"What's with her?" Storm whispered to Rose, giving Rainstorm another quick glance.

"She is worried about the others." Rose whispered back. "I tried to cheer her up but nothing seems to be working." She added with a frown. The two of them looked back at Rainstorm.

"I can hear you, you know." Rainstorm muttered.

"Look, I'm sure that they will be back soon, who knows maybe they're already on their way back." Storm said, giving Rainstorm a small smile. "You really should eat, it might make you feel better."

"I already told you I'm not hungry!" Rainstorm hissed at him. "And I don't need you two trying to cheer me up!"

"But-" Rose started before Rainstorm stormed out of the dining hall, towards her room.

I don't need their help, I don't need anyone's help. I was fine with being all by myself. I never asked for all this. Rainstorm thought furiously, as she stormed past the other rooms and rushed into the room she and Fury had stayed in, slamming the door behind her. She rushed into a corner and curled up into a tight coil, her head resting on her tail. Then she took a deep breath, and her eyes began to tear up as she began to cry.

All she could think about was Fury, her mind spinning with thoughts of what could have happened to them. Then her mind began to slow down as she remembered the day they had met. How Fury seemed so mad at her, yet even his fiery gaze seemed to soften when he looked at her. She knew that only he could make her feel better, only he could comfort her. She needed him just as much as he needed her.

Rainstorm looked up as she heard a knock at the door.

"Go away!" Rainstorm yelled in between sobs.

"Look, all we want to do is help." Rose insisted, knocking on the door again.

"I said go away!" Rainstorm hissed, throwing the first thing she could grab at the door. There was a sigh at the door and after a while things started to get quiet again.

Rainstorm layed there, weeping until her sobs finally quieted as she began to fall into a dreamless sleep. After a while she began to slowly wake up, slowly opening her eyes. The room was almost pitch black, and the air felt awfully cold. Rainstorm shivered as she raised her head and squinted, trying to get her eyes to adjust to the darkness.

Why is it so cold in here? She thought, her eyes slowly beginning to adjust to the darkness. She looked around until she stopped, seeing something moving around on the other side of the room.

"Who's there?" Rainstorm muttered, squinting to try and get a better look at whatever was in the room with her.

"Oh, you're finally awake." The figure said in an unsettlingly calm voice.

"Who are you? What are you doing here?" Rainstorm asked, before letting out a gasp as she finally was able to see the figure clearly.

"I believe you know who I am." Snowstorm sneered, giving Rainstorm a cold glare. Rainstorm rushed over to the door and tried to force it open, but it seemed to have been sealed by a sheet of ice.

"Help! Somebody help me!" Rainstorm shouted, pushing against the door one final time before turning around and facing Snowstorm with a hiss.

"Tsk tsk, silly little dragonet, nobody can hear you." Snowstorm hissed.

"You need to leave before the others get back." Rainstorm hissed, preparing to shoot a burst of electricity at the banished queen. Her mind immediately began to fill up with thoughts of Fury.

What would he do in this situation? Well he would probably just start attacking without a plan. Rainstorm thought, before her thoughts were interrupted by the snickering coming from Snowstorm.

"That is probably something he would do, or at least it would have been." Snowstorm said with a smirk.

"What the, how did you do that? And what do you mean by 'would have been'?" Rainstorm gasped, backing away from the door.

"Oh did Whirlwind not tell everyone about my other little gift. Oh wait, he didn't get the chance to." Snowstorm sneered. "I can hear the thoughts of those that have been in contact with any descendant of mine."

"You've been quite the pest you know? If it hadn't been for you Fury wouldn't be trying to be good, and I could have had a son that wasn't such a disappointment like the rest." Snowstorm hissed, her eyes giving off a faint glow.

"Fury is not a disappointment!" Rainstorm hissed, unleashing a blast of electricity from her mouth, barely missing Snowstorm.

"He won't be, once I get rid of you. Then I'll have him kill that pathetic excuse for a king, Bolt." Snowstorm hissed, spreading her wings out.

"He will never do that!" Rainstorm hissed, letting out another blast of electricity, this time managing to graze Snowstorm's side. Snowstorm let out a little hiss, looking at the wound before looking back up at Rainstorm.

"That's cute, you really think you can stop me?" Snowstorm sneered, moving closer to Rainstorm, her tail twitching in annoyance. She whipped her tail across Rainstorm's snout, the force of the impact flinging her back. Panicked, Rainstorm fired a burst of energy at the wall of ice blocking the door, trying to melt it. Snowstorm let out a laugh.

"That wall is made from eternal ice, it would take an incredible amount of heat to get it to melt." Snowstorm sneered, whipping Rainstorm across her side time and time again, moving her away from the door.

"Rainstorm, are you ok in there?" Rose asked from the other side of the door.

"Help me." Rainstorm tried to choke out, trying to get to the door before being pulled back by Snowstorm. Rainstorm fired another blast at Snowstorm, hitting her on the side of her face, before using what little energy she had left to leap towards the door.

"Help! It's Snowstorm, she's here!" Rainstorm shouted at the top of her lungs, before firing another blast at Snowstorm.

"What! Hold on, I can help!" Rose shouted in a panic.

She doesn't know about the ice. She'll never be able to get through in time.

Rainstorm realized.

"Any last words?" Snowstorm sneered, her jaws opening, as she got ready to unleash a burst of energy at Rainstorm. Right before she could deal the final blow, a loud noise could be heard from the other side of the door. Both Rainstorm and Snowstorm stared at the door as a small little hole began to burn through.

"That's not possible!" Snowstorm hissed, glaring at the door, before looking back at Rainstorm. Rainstorm stared in awe at the hole that continued to grow until she could see Rose on the other side. Rose was letting out a continuous beam of energy which glowed an unnaturally bright pink. The energy was branching out across the door and seemed to be melting through the ice with no problems.

"Nobody has had that amount of energy in centuries!" Snowstorm hissed, letting out a burst of freezing air, trying to stop Rose from getting in. But no matter how hard she tried, she could not get the ice to reform. Snowstorm let out a roar of fury, glaring at Rainstorm, who despite all her wounds, managed to get back up, a fierce look in her eyes.

"You underestimated us. We are not just weak little dragonets. We have more power than you ever will. You had your chance and you let it go to waste. Now we're going to put you back in your place." Rainstorm hissed, unleashing a volley of electric burst at Snowstorm, searing her scales. Snowstorm let out another roar of fury and pain, before collapsing onto the ground. There was a small hint of fear in her eyes as she looked back at the door which Rose had almost burned down completely.

"No, I will not go back to that awful chamber!" Snowstorm hissed, leaping at Rainstorm. "This is my kingdom! I will not let it be taken from me again!" Snowstorm dove through the door and flew as fast as she could out of the palace.

"Good riddens." Rainstorm muttered, before collapsing onto the ground, a pool of blood slowly growing around her.

"Rainstorm!" Rose shouted, rushing into the room, stopping right in front of her face. "Come on, come on. Stay with me. Don't you die on me!"

"Tell Fury that I owe him my life, for finally being that good thing in my life." Rainstorm muttered, her eyes slowly closing, before everything went black.

CHAPTER

17

Bolt, Sky, and Fury got to the palace door, a smile on their faces.

"I'm glad that's over with." Sky said with a sigh. She looked over at Bolt, who was still messing with the amulet. "Why do you keep messing with that thing?" she asked, giving him a confused smile.

"I don't know, it's just that something doesn't feel right. I don't know what, but I think the amulet is trying to get me to notice something." Bolt replied, before letting go of the amulet with a frustrated groan.

"It's probably saying 'stop using me to mess with others' and I think you should listen to it." Fury said with a smirk.

"Oh stop it, you and I both know he didn't do it on purpose." Sky snickered, nudging Fury with her tail. Bolt nodded, giving them an apologetic smile.

"I just hope we didn't miss anything." Sky muttered, a worried expression spreading across her face.

"Oh I'm sure we didn't. But I bet you one of us here is really missing a certain dragonet back at the palace." Bolt snickered, giving Fury a teasing nudge. Fury hissed, glaring at Bolt, but his gaze softened shortly after.

"Do you think she missed me?" Fury asked, giving Bolt and Sky a hopeful smile. They stopped, hearing something in the distance.

"Do you guys hear the sound of wings flapping?" Bolt asked the others, a puzzled expression sweeping over his face.

"Yeah, I wonder who it could be?" Sky muttered, seeming to be deep in thought. All of a sudden they were knocked back by a large gust of wind, as a large dragon sped past them, before bursting out of the palace.

"Was that who I thought it was?" Sky said nervously, looking at Bolt and Fury.

"No way, couldn't have been. She wouldn't dare show her face here." Bolt stuttered, trying to sound convincing. Then they jumped as they heard Rose shouting for help.

"Well this isn't good." Fury hissed, rushing to the sound of his sister's voice, Bolt and Sky following shortly behind. As they flew to where they had heard Rose, Bolt's head began to fill up with anxious thoughts.

Was that really Snowstorm? What was she doing here? She must have been looking for me right? Oh, I do hope nobody got hurt. Bolt's mind spun with everything that might have happened. When they finally got to Rose they let out a gasp as they saw Rainstorm, laying in a heap on the ground, blood pooling around her. Sky wrapped her wings around Bolt, tears beginning to form in her eyes.

Oh no, Snowstorm attacked Rainstorm. But why? Why would she go after Rainstorm. Fury must be heartbroken. Bolt thought, glancing at Fury, who sure enough had a fierce look in his eyes, his entire body shaking with rage. *I wonder how he is going to take it.* Bolt wondered, staring at his brother. Sky slowly went up to

Rainstorm and lifted her chin up with her tail. She leaned over and stopped right in front of her, before putting her head back down with a sigh.

"She's still breathing. But she's going to need help because of how much blood she is losing." Sky muttered quietly, giving Fury an apologetic look. Fury seemed to calm down for a moment, before his tail started buzzing with energy as it started to shake. He turned to face Bolt with a glare of pure hatred in his eyes.

"This is all your fault." Fury said in a low hiss. Bolt's eyes widened hearing this.

"My fault!? How was this my fault!?" Bolt demanded, glaring at his brother.

"If it wasn't for you and that stupid amulet we would never have gotten trapped back in that cave. We would have been here and we could have stopped Snowstorm!" Fury hissed, his tail beginning to glow a deep red. Sky tried to get in between them.

"Now, there is no need to fight. Bolt didn't do that on purpose and you know it. The only one at fault is Snowstorm." Sky insisted, trying to calm Fury down. Fury hissed at her and pushed her back, knocking her into the wall.

"Hey! What was that for!" Bolt hissed, pushing Fury back with more force, and accidentally cutting him with the barb on his tail. Fury let out another hissed and looked at the deep cut that was in his tail, before looking back at Bolt.

"I'm sorry!" Bolt said nervously, trying to help Fury up.

"You're gonna be." Fury hissed, ready to lunge at Bolt, before being stopped by his sister.

"Will you two quit fighting! Can't you see that Rainstorm is hurt! Why don't you make yourselves useful and go try to find help." Rose hissed, glaring at the both of them. Shocked by Rose's outburst, Bolt and Fury gave each other one last glare and went off to find Storm. As they left, Rose helped Sky up, and the two of them went over to Rainstorm.

"Can you heal her?" Sky asked, a worried expression on her face.

"I can try." Rose stuttered, placing her tail on Rainstorm. She closed her eyes as her tail began to glow that familiar pink. Little branches of energy began to flow out of her tail and started spreading across Rainstorm, slowly healing her wounds. The two of them watched as the final cuts across Rainstorm's body began to close up. Then they got quiet, waiting for any sign that it worked. They jumped as Rainstorm took a deep breath and began coughing. Her eyes slowly opened to see both Rose and Sky smiling at her, with tears going down their snouts. The two of them wrapped their wings around Rainstorm, pulling her into a tight hug.

"We thought you were gone." Sky muttered, tightening the hug.

"I might not make it if I can't breathe." Rainstorm managed to choke out.

"Oh sorry about that." Sky said apologetically, both her and Rose letting go. Rainstorm took another deep breath before giving them both a big smile.

"You came back! I thought something had happened to you! Wait, is Fury here?" Rainstorm said, her eyes lightning up with joy.

"Yeah but he got really mad at Bolt and thinks that what happened to you was his fault. He would have attacked Bolt if I hadn't stopped him." Rose muttered.

"He-He was about to attack Boly." Rainstorm stuttered, backing away.

If he was willing to attack his own brother, what's gonna keep him from attacking me? Rainstorm thought, her mind beginning to fill up with fear. *Then all that I've done to try to get him to be good would be all for nothing. Maybe it would just be for the best if I wasn't around him, so that if anything does happen to me he won't get mad and attack someone.* Her mind continued filling up with these thoughts, until she heard flapping coming from down the hall.

"They're coming back! I can't wait for them to see that you're alright!" Rose said, a smile spreading across her face. Rainstorm's mind began going through all the things she had been through after she had met Fury and the others. She closed her eyes and took a deep breath.

"No. They can't know that I survived." Rainstorm muttered, her eyes slowly opening back up.

"Wait, what?" Sky said, puzzled by what Rainstorm had said. "Why not?"

"If Fury was willing to attack his own brother because of me, then I believe it would be for the best for him to think I was gone." Rainstorm sighed.

"But-" Rose started before being cut off by Rainstorm.

"Tell them that by the time you healed my wounds, it was already too late." Rainstorm sighed. Sky opened her mouth to try to convince Rainstorm, but then closed it and gave her a small nod. Rainstorm gave a small smile, before laying back down.

"Are you sure this is what you want?" Sky whispered, giving Rainstorm a frown. Rainstorm nodded, before looking at Rose, whose eyes were beginning to fill with tears again.

"Will we ever see each other again?" Rose choked out, trying to hold back her tears.

"Eventually, I will return when I see it as necessary." Rainstorm said with a smile, before closing her eyes. Not long after Bolt and Fury came into the room, along with Storm by their side. They stopped as they saw Sky and Rose in front of Rainstorm, seeing the tears roll down their snouts.

"Is she?" Storm began, stopping when Sky and Rose gave them a small nod. He went over beside Rose and put his wings around her, Bolt doing the same with Sky. Fury just stared at Rainstorm, slowly backing away.

"No." Fury stuttered "She can't be." He wrapped his wings around himself and buried his head between them. Everyone looked over at Fury, whose body was shaking.

"I'm so sorry." Bolt stuttered, slowly moving up to Fury.

"No." Fury muttered, before going quiet. Then he raised his head, tears streaming down his snout, his eyes glowing a bright red, as he glared at Bolt.

"This is all your fault!" Fury roared, flaring his wings out, as they began to crackle with energy. "I'm going to kill you!" He roared again leaping at Bolt, knocking him over, trying to sink his teeth into his neck.

"Bolt!" Sky cried, rushing over to help Bolt, only to be forced back by the spike on Furys tail. Bolt let out a roar of pain as Fury sank his fangs into his side. Bolt pushed Fury off of him, glaring at him.

"We can talk about this!" Bolt shouted, trying to reason with his brother.

"The time to talk is over! You let the only thing that ever mattered to me die! And now I'm going to make you pay!" Fury roared, firing a large blast of electricity that glowed the color of blood at Bolt, hitting him square in the chest. Bolt stumbled back, before looking down at his amulet, which was glowing a bright fiery red. Bolt looked back up at his enraged brother.

"I don't want to hurt you, but you're not giving me much of a choice!" Bolt shouted, doing the best he could to try to get his brother under control. Bolt lept to the side, barely avoiding another large blast of energy.

"Too bad we don't have the same idea." Fury hissed, before unleashing a volley of electric bursts at Bolt. Bolt tried to avoid them but got hit by a few of the bursts. Bolt winced, and looked back down at the amulet. Bolt took a deep breath and let out a sigh.

"I'm sorry." Bolt muttered, closing his eyes before letting out a large burst of energy. As he did this the amulet began to heat up the air around them and a beam of fire shot out of his mouth, fusing with the electricity. Fury's eyes widened and he let out a roar of pain as the burst hit him, creating a small explosion. When Bolt opened his eyes, he saw his brother leaning against a wall, badly burned and cut up. Bolt approached his brother, who was trying to push himself back up. Bolt stopped right in front of Fury and glared at him.

"You have given me no choice. Fury, you are hereby banished from the kingdom." Bolt hissed.

"This isn't over." Fury hissed. "I will return, next time with an army of my own. And I will have my revenge and then, only then, will I finally be happy again." Fury hissed in pain as he got off the wall and flew out of the palace.

EPILOGUE

"What happened then?" one of the kids asked the father, looking up at him with fear in his eyes.

"Yeah what happened? Did Fury ever come back?" the other child added, looking up at their father.

"Well, nobody knows. But what we do know is that we have no need to worry about what will happen, because we know that there are others that would do anything to save others." The father said with a smile. The boys let out a big yawn as their eyes struggled to stay open.

"Are they really going to protect us?" one of the boys said, before letting out another yawn.

"Yes, I am positive they will be able to protect us, all we need to do is trust them." The father said with a smile, before letting out a yawn himself. The father got up and looked up at the night sky as shooting stars cut through the sky. He smiled knowing that this place they called home would always have protectors.

"Boy why don't you head into our tent. It is getting quite late and I believe all of us deserve a good night's sleep. I will join you soon." The father said, looking back at his kids, smiling as he saw that they had already fallen fast asleep. The father carefully scooped them up, trying not to wake them up. He opened up the tent and laid them down in their sleeping bags, quietly tucking them in. He bent over and gave each of them a kiss on the forehead.

"Sweet dreams." He whispered. He looked back out at the surrounding land around them. He looked up as he heard the roar of a dragon above. He smiled as he saw the faint glint of blue that was moving around in the sky.

"We wish you the best of luck, we all are depending on you." He whispered, before heading into the tent and zipping the door closed. Then he turned off the light as the sound of crickets began to grow, before laying down, and falling asleep.